A FATE WORSE THAN DEATH

A HOLLYWOOD MYSTERY PREQUEL

D1648809

BRITT LIND

Designed and distributed by Bublish, Inc.

ISBN: 978-1-647043-92-6 (paperback)
ISBN: 978-1-647043-89-6 (eBook)

Praise for *Deception: A Hollywood Mystery*

"A thrilling page-turner about a group of flawed, yet compelling characters caught in a cesspool of greed and ruthless ambition behind the scenes in Hollywood. I couldn't wait to find out the ending while simultaneously wishing the book wouldn't end."

Lara Wickman—Writer, Producer, Actress

"…the story takes some refreshingly unexpected turns, picking a path through genre clichés and keeping readers guessing. The author has an easy writing style and a cinematic grasp of pace. Fans of silver screen crime should approve, as, in many respects, this reads like the novelization of a movie."

Kirkus Reviews

"If you want to read a book that offers romance, suspense, detective work, intrigue, and feels like you're watching a movie, then this is your book. I highly recommend it"

Andreas Michaelides—Writer, Reviewer, Blogger, and Natural Health Educator

"*Deception* is a gritty rendering of the classic battle between good and evil played out in the milieu of Hollywood. As an actor herself, Britt is ably qualified to explore and articulate the disappointment and heartache of fame-obsessed performers as they struggle to "make it" in an unforgiving industry where fame is illusive and disappointment can lead to murder."

Tony Eldridge—Executive Producer—
The Equalizer I, The Equalizer II

Praise for *Learning How to Fly*

(Beverly Hills Book Award Winner)

"Britt Lind's journey to find her ultimate calling (a voice for the animals) is filled with highs and lows on her road to Hollywood, and you will want to keep turning the page."

Sylva Kelegian—Actress, writer, and award-winning author
of *God Spelled Backwards* and *The Dolphin Princess*

"*Learning How to Fly* is the inspiring story of a fellow activist who has hung in there through thick and thin for all of the 32 years I've known her. Fighting vivisection is a hard road and it takes both courage and incredible patience to stay in the battle. But Britt found a way to stay on course and still fulfill her passion for acting. Readers will find this book entertaining and humorous, but it's also her journey that provides guidance on how one can find their own way to a meaningful life."

With Respect for all Life—Chris DeRose—Founder
and President of Last Chance for Animals and
author of an autobiography, *In Your Face*

"As a young starlet, Britt Lind was a beauty who was cast in a Clint Eastwood movie and found happiness being married to a television producer and acting and raising a baby girl. But in a flash, her marriage ended, riches vanished, the house was foreclosed on and her career crumbled. Britt's story of disappearing success is poignant and unforgettable, and by the time she is beaten down in Hollywood and heads for New York with visions of Broadway, you cannot help but cheer for her and the animals she has dedicated her life to saving. This is a heartfelt, timeless story of shining on to create a life filled with love, beauty and triumph."

Janette Turner—Writer, director and author of the forthcoming memoir *Magazine Crush: My Life as a Cosmo Addict*

"These are the adventures of an innocent young girl from Norway, thrust into American culture, driven by a passionate ambition to be an actress in a ruthlessly unpredictable and sexist industry. Britt navigated through a life of obstacles, betrayals and disappointments with courageous resolve, a resolve deeply rooted in a firm moral foundation and strengthened by a deep compassion and a fiery desire to end the suffering of animals."

Captain Paul Watson—Founder of The Sea Shepherd Conservation Society and author of several books including: *Sea Shepherd: My Fight for Whales and Seals, Seal Wars: Twenty-Five Years on the Front Lines with the Harp Seals,* and *Ocean Warrior: My Battle to End the Illegal Slaughter on the High Seas*

To Rod Allison who was my brother in spirit,
always looking out for me, always with a ready smile.
He broke my heart when he left this earth for heaven, where
I'm sure the angels welcomed him as one of their own.

*A father is neither an anchor to hold us
back nor a sail to take us there,
but is a guiding light whose love
shows us the way.*

—Anonymous

CHAPTER ONE

Nine-year-old Rosemaria Baker sat entranced, staring up at Ingrid Bergman's perfect features and glowing, alabaster complexion on the giant movie screen. Ingrid's face seemed to barely move, and yet she so convincingly conveyed her confusion and fear as the gas lamps on the stairs flickered and sounds from the attic caused Ingrid to doubt her sanity. Olivia Baker, Rosemaria's mother, sat beside her, completely enraptured by the charismatic actress and her villain of a husband who was trying to drive her insane. Neither Rosemaria nor Olivia moved or spoke as the story unfolded until, finally, Joseph Cotton stepped in to expose the malicious Charles Boyer as a scheming liar and fraud.

Rosemaria sighed contentedly as the credits rolled, but she was ready to leave. Hunger pangs reminded her that her mother had promised to take her to McDonald's for lunch. Olivia, still enthralled by the movie, took her daughter's hand and led her out into the sunlight. She had allowed Rosemaria to skip school and come with her to the budget theater in Simi Valley that periodically showed classic movies. The theater was close to their neighborhood, and Olivia spent many an afternoon losing herself in a world of movie make-believe. If she found out that one of her favorites was showing somewhere else in the LA area, she would sometimes make a special trip to see it. After all, as an actress herself, this was really research, not just entertainment. Ingrid Bergman was Olivia's idol and ideal. She didn't fool herself into thinking that she was as beautiful as Ingrid. With her auburn hair, green eyes, and freckles, Olivia knew she couldn't compete with Ingrid's stunning, Nordic good looks, but she felt confident that as an actress she had that same subtle acting technique through which she could portray any emotion effortlessly, without resorting to cheap theatrics.

They walked to their car in the parking lot, and Olivia strapped her daughter into the back seat. She spoke to Rosemaria in a voice tinged with regret. "Ingrid was twenty-nine when she made that film and had made other movies before that one. I'm already thirty and I still haven't done anything important after seven years of knocking on doors."

"It's not too late, Mama," Rosemaria piped up. She knew only too well how desperately her mother wanted to make it as an actress. "You'll be beautiful for a long, long time still."

Olivia bent over and kissed her daughter on the top of her head. "Thank you, my sweet girl. All I can do is keep trying."

Rosemaria waited a few moments so she wouldn't seem too eager to change the subject before she asked, "Can we go to McDonald's now?"

Olivia laughed. "Fillet, fries, and a coke?"

"Yeah!" Rosemaria laughed with her.

* * * *

Olivia pulled into the driveway of their ranch-style house, which looked almost identical to the other houses on the block. She clicked open the garage door and saw that her husband was home. He had pulled his gray Honda inside. Maybe that meant he had the day off from work tomorrow. She parked her own yellow Mazda beside the Honda.

Rosemaria unclicked her belt, full of childish glee. "Daddy's home!"

She ran to the door and burst into the kitchen where Steven Baker—tall, handsome, with light-brown hair that was starting to get a little gray in the sideburns—was leaning against the counter with a can of Budweiser in his hand. He immediately put it down at the sight of his daughter. Rosemaria flew to her father, who then lifted her high in the air and hugged her close. "What's going on, little girl? Why are you home so late from school?"

"Movie. Mom took me to a movie, and it was really scary. And then we went to McDonald's."

He looked up as Olivia came through the door. "Movie, huh? During a school day?"

Olivia gave him a peck on the cheek as she walked by on her way to the bedroom. "Playing hooky one day won't hurt. I'll tell the teacher she had a slight cold."

Steven kept Rosemaria trapped in a bear hug. "I guess one day of missing class won't keep you out of college."

Rosemaria laughed. "Maybe I'll be an actress instead. School is boring."

Olivia turned around and waved her finger in the air. "Oh no, you're going to have something to fall back on. Not like me." She disappeared down the hallway.

Steven poured the rest of his beer down the sink. "Since you've been sitting all this time, how about we go to the park and do some batting practice?"

"Will you tell me about your day?"

"Of course."

"All the gory details?"

Steven shook his head. "I'll save those for when you're a little older. Maybe next year." He patted her on her back, sending her on her way down the hall. "Go get changed. You don't want to let the boys outplay you."

"Never!" She raced to her room.

* * * *

"Were you scared, Daddy? Did you think that someone was still hiding in the house?" Rosemaria held her mac and cheese on her fork an inch from her mouth, waiting for his response. The dinner table was where she liked to drill her father about his day as a robbery-homicide detective, even though her mother would rather skip hearing about any of it.

Her father stopped chewing long enough to answer. "Well, we knew this was the house where the three robbers stored a lot of the stolen property, and we had a tip that one of them lived there. So, we were careful and cleared every room as we went through the house."

"Cleared! That means make sure nobody is there!"

Steven smiled at his daughter, a pint-sized mirror image of her mother, and took another bite of mac and cheese. He chewed and spoke with his mouth full. "Exactly. You're learning."

Olivia watched them both and shook her head. "Are you sure all of this cops-and-robbers stuff isn't going to give you bad dreams, honey?"

Rosemaria looked surprised. "I never have bad dreams. I like knowing what Daddy's doing and where he is. Then I don't have to worry about him."

Olivia shook her head, resigned. "Okay, if you say so."

Rosemaria took a big gulp of her grape juice. "And it sounds like fun, too."

Her father's expression turned serious. "I guess it can seem that way if you think that what I'm doing is like on TV, where bad guys are actors and don't really die when they get shot. But in real life, people don't always get up when they get hurt, and that means us cops as well as the bad guys."

"Honey, now you're scaring her." She looked at her daughter. "Who wants some ice cream?"

"I do! I'll help!" Rosemaria jumped up from the table just as the phone on the wall near the kitchen counter rang. She reached up to answer it and lifted the receiver to her ear. "Baker residence," she said in a very business-like manner. "Yes, she's here." She handed the receiver to her mom, who grabbed it and waited anxiously a split second before speaking.

"Hello." Olivia listened intently. Then her face lit up in a wide grin. "I did? When? Okay… Okay… Thank you… Thank you so much!" She hung up the phone and faced her husband and daughter, who were looking at her expectantly.

"You know that play I auditioned for last week, the one at the Mallory Playhouse? I got the part!"

Rosemaria grabbed her mother around her waist and squeezed. "I'm so happy for you, Mommy!"

Steven stood up and enveloped his wife in a bear hug. "I'm so proud of you! Congratulations!"

"It's Equity, honey! I'll get paid. It's not just 99-seat waiver. It's Union!" Olivia went to the freezer, opened it up, and grabbed a big container of ice cream. She held it high. "Let's eat till we burst!"

Rosemaria was already grabbing spoons out of the drawer.

CHAPTER TWO

The rain was coming down in a deluge. Sergeant Lyle Hirschberg was driving. He could hardly see through the windshield as the wipers tried their best to keep up with the onslaught. Steven was sitting shotgun and squinting through the darkness to try to figure out exactly where their turnoff was. "I think it's the next block," he said.

The two men had been working together for three years, and Steven considered himself lucky to have Lyle for a partner. Lyle didn't look like the typical TV detective with his slight, unmuscular frame and his thinning red hair, pale complexion, and nervous demeaner. But Steven had found him to be a dogged investigator and unfailingly dependable in a clutch. They were headed for the house of Edgar Escochea, whose nephew Manny Sanchez had just been paroled. Sanchez was supposed to be staying in a halfway house, but their intel told them otherwise. They had merely wanted to talk to him about one of his former buddies, Lester Chavez, who had taken part in a gas station holdup with Sanchez but had escaped capture and conviction. Now, if what they had heard was true—that Sanchez was hanging around with Escochea, another convicted felon—his parole could be revoked. The two detectives would like to avoid that. They'd rather get their hands on Chavez and get him off the streets. Steven was eager to get Sanchez down to the station, interview him, and then get home. Tonight, was the opening of Olivia's play, and he had promised Rosemaria that she would be his date. It was already half past five, and he needed to be at the theater with his daughter by eight. He hoped Sanchez would be a willing witness and not cause any delays. They had the parole violation to hold over his head, so he should be willing to spill his guts about whatever he knew.

Lyle made a right turn, and Steven started reading off the house numbers. "Forty-two fifty-eight. It must be the next one, with the broken fence."

Lyle drove by the house slowly. There was a dim light inside. He parked half a block away, and they both pulled their Glocks out of their holsters, checked them, reholstered, stepped out of the unmarked car and into the pouring rain. They walked quickly down the street, eyes on their surroundings, to the front porch of the dilapidated house, where they found a bit of shelter from the downpour. They peered in the front window and saw no one. They could barely make out a table in the kitchen that seemed to be laden with piles of small plastic packets of a white powdery substance.

Steven spoke first. "No warrant. We can't go in."

"I guess we didn't hear a cry for help either."

The light in the kitchen went out. "I'll go right. You go left." Steven said.

Lyle took out his Glock and flashlight and stepped off the porch. Steven did the same. They proceeded to slowly make their way around either side of the house. The adrenalin of both men was surging. Rain and sweat were mingling on their faces as they approached the backyard.

Steven heard movement by the back door. He noted a thick rake handle leaning on the far side of the back door by an overflowing garbage can. Suddenly a shadow streaked from behind a pile of wood and broken furniture and raced down Lyle's side of the house to the front. Steven's flashlight caught another man following and he heard Lyle grunt as if he'd hit the ground. He rounded the corner of the back of the house and saw Lyle on the ground, struggling with a middle-aged Hispanic man for the control of his gun. A shot rang out. Steven grabbed the rake handle, took two steps toward the men on the ground, and, after waiting for a clear shot, swung with all his might at the Hispanic man's head. He went down-and-out like a lead balloon.

Steven quickly knelt beside Lyle. "You okay?"

Lyle grimaced in pain. "I twisted my damn shoulder. I can't believe I let the bastard get the better of me."

Steven took out his radio and clicked it on. "Officers in need of assistance and ambulance at forty-two sixty Laurel Street. And issue a BOLO for Manny Sanchez, last seen fleeing the scene of an attack on an officer at the same address. Copy?"

The radio crackled. "Copy that. Units are on the way."

He clicked off and looked down at Edgar Escochea. "He'll live."

* * * *

Steven was in the waiting area of the Good Samaritan Hospital, where Lyle was being treated for a pulled muscle in his arm. The doctor had told him that Lyle should be back in working order in two weeks. Steven used his cell to call home.

Rosemaria answered. "Mommy's really mad at you. She had to call and ask Matt and Carol to take me to the theater."

"You're home by yourself?" Steven became alarmed.

"It's only for about fifteen minutes, then they'll be here. I'm not a baby, you know."

"Even so." He sighed. "I'm sorry, but I'm going to be late getting to the theater. Lyle and I had to arrest somebody."

Rosemaria's entire demeanor changed. "Did they do something really bad? Did they rob a bank or something? Was it dangerous?"

Steven mumbled to himself, "What have I done to create a child so excited at the thought of chasing criminals?"

"What Daddy?"

"Nothing. Tell the Claytons that I'll be about half an hour late and to save me a seat beside you."

"Okay. Then you can tell me more when I see you."

Steven had to laugh in spite of himself. "Yes, I'll tell you all about it. All the gory details. But don't tell your mom."

"I promise!"

He hung up and called the station. "It's Baker. Could you connect me with Farber?" He waited. "Yeah, Lieutenant, is it okay if I fill out the paperwork tomorrow? If I don't get to my wife's play, she'll give me grief for the next month… Great. Yeah, first thing in the morning." He hung up as Lyle came down the hallway, one arm in a sling.

"Did you find out if Escochea is still with us?" Lyle asked.

"Yeah, he has a concussion, and his eye almost left its socket, but they'll move him to the prison infirmary in a couple of days."

"Did you see him wrestling with me? If you hadn't hit him, the next shot could've killed me. I'll be goin' to the gym with you as soon as I'm out of this thing." He looked over at Steven, who was stifling a laugh. "What?"

Lyle's aversion to working out was well-known, but Steven was all innocence. "Nothing." They walked side by side down the hall and out to the parking lot, Lyle mumbling under his breath and Steven doing his best to show sympathy.

* * * *

Steven used all his driving skills to weave in and out of Friday night traffic. His years hauling ass down freeways and city streets as a patrolman were serving him well as he headed up the 5 freeway to Burbank. Through sheer luck and clean living, the traffic gods decided to give him every break, and he made it to his seat just as the lights in the theater were going down. He whispered his apologies to the Claytons, their next-door neighbors who were always willing to help out in a pinch, gave Rosemaria a kiss on the top of her head, and then the play began. He had seen his wife onstage before in small productions but never in a professional play in a five-hundred-seat theater. He was surprised at how nervous he felt for her.

His wife was the first to appear onstage as the play opened. Apparently, hers was the leading role. She played a put-upon housewife, constantly demeaned by her lout of a husband as she went about serving him. The play was a comedy, and Olivia immediately garnered laughs as her character bravely attempted to overcome her husband's demands and put-downs. She had a scene with an actress who played her older sister, who was hilarious in her role as an interviewer at a job agency. The back and forth between the aggressive interviewer and the frightened housewife made for some pathos in the scene as well as a great deal of laughs. Steven didn't know much about acting, but it was obvious that his wife had immense talent and a confident stage presence. By intermission he had relaxed and was thoroughly enjoying himself.

As the lights came up, Rosemaria looked up at him. "She's really good isn't she, Daddy?"

"She's better than good. She's incredible." And he meant it.

He let the Claytons take Rosemaria out to the lobby for refreshments. Meanwhile his mind drifted back to the first time he'd seen Olivia. He'd been driving on the 101 freeway around twelve midnight, on his way home to his apartment in the San Fernando Valley and had seen a young woman in a summer dress and headscarf stranded on the side of the freeway with a flat tire. She was reaching into the trunk trying to pull out her spare and was actually about to change the tire that was on the side facing the freeway. He made a split-second decision to stop before the crazy woman killed herself. He pulled over and backed up to where her car was parked. She observed him closely, not as if he were a rescuer but as if she were wondering who this crazy person was getting out of his car and walking toward her. She looked like she was about to leap back into her car and lock the doors. He held out his badge and reassured her he was a cop and was there to help. After her fear subsided, she collapsed against the car with relief, and her eyes filled with tears. Her scarf slid off and flew with the wind across the freeway.

"Now, now," Steven said, trying to comfort her, and at the same time realizing that she was one of the most beautiful women he'd ever seen. "I have a police radio in my car. I'll call a tow truck and get your tire changed. You can wait in my car, or yours if that makes you feel safer."

The woman hesitated then said, "I'll get in my car if that's okay."

"Sure, no problem."

He walked back to his car and called the tow truck, wondering how he could find out if the woman was married and if it was kosher for him to somehow finagle a date. He sat behind the wheel and watched her sitting, waiting without moving, and he then saw her head fall forward on the steering wheel and stay there. He fought the impulse to go check on her. When the tow truck showed up, he badged the guy and knocked on the woman's window. She had been sound asleep and awoke with a start. She rubbed her eyes and rolled down the window.

"I don't have a Triple A card."

Steven waved it off. "No problem. Police emergency. I'll take care of it."

"I don't want you to pay."

"Don't worry. It's police business. But ma'am, I don't think you're in any condition to drive. You were sound asleep just now."

She bit her lip. "I worked the late shift at an answering service, and I'm beat."

"Why don't I have the driver tow your car to your house and he can change the tire there?"

"That sounds really expensive! Are you sure you don't have to pay?"

"It'll be taken care of."

Steven spoke briefly to the driver, then the woman followed him to his car, and they waited while her car was being hooked up to the tow truck. They drove in tandem to North Hollywood where she lived, not too far from him, in an apartment with her roommate. After the tow truck driver had changed her tire, saying goodnight to her in the car had taken two hours. They hadn't so much as touched, but both knew something special was happening between them.

Paying for the tow and tire change had emptied out his wallet, but he hadn't cared.

He smiled now, remembering the loony, lovestruck kid he'd been.

The Claytons came back to claim their seats and he stood to let them by. Rosemaria slid past him and plopped down in her seat just as the lights began to go down. "This half is even better, Daddy. I know because I ran lines with Mommy."

"She's lucky to have such a good reader," he whispered back.

She put her forefinger up to her mouth to hush him, and the second half of the play began.

* * * *

"Did you hear the applause?" Oliva was gloriously in her element as she waltzed around the tiny dressing room. "It washed over me like a tidal wave! Comedies don't usually get standing O's, but we got one anyway!"

Steven and Rosemaria stood aside as cast members and friends, including Matt and Carol, came to revel in the excitement of opening night. They showered Olivia with compliments, and she drank them up like a desert wanderer who'd just come upon a lush oasis. She looked over at her husband and child.

"We're having a cast party at Chez Nous." She hesitated. "Would the two of you like to come or…"

Rosemaria looked up at her father. "Could we come for a little while, Daddy?"

"No, I think it's best to get you home, sweetheart."

"Okay, I'll see you two tomorrow then. Don't wait up for me!" Olivia gave Steven a peck on the cheek and wrapped her arms around Rosemaria. "Love you, baby." And then she turned back to her friends and continued to bask in the afterglow of a successful opening.

Steven took his daughter's hand, and they walked down the back hallway and out to the parking lot. They were both subdued.

"Mommy is happiest when she's acting isn't she, Daddy?"

"That's true, honey. That's where her heart is."

"Isn't her heart with us?"

He laughed, swooped his daughter up in his arms, and held her tight for a few moments. "First and foremost, honey, first and foremost!" He set her down, took out his keys and opened the car door. He reached inside and pulled up the knob to unlock the back door. Rosemaria climbed in and attached her seatbelt. She did not look convinced. He sat down in the driver's seat then turned around and looked at his slightly crestfallen daughter. "Have I ever lied to you?"

"No."

"Then how about we go home and celebrate Mommy's great performance with hot chocolate, and I'll tell you all about what happened tonight when some criminals came after Lyle and me and your father had to save the day?"

That lit Rosemaria up like a Christmas tree. "Yeah! And tell me all the gory details!"

"You got it!"

He pulled out of the parking lot feeling like the luckiest guy in the world.

CHAPTER THREE

Even to Rosemaria and her best friend—blond, blue-eyed Priscilla Lovett—who had also grown up in the oppressive heat of Simi Valley, this spring day was unbearable. They sat outside Garden Grove Elementary School, having found a bit of welcome shade under a tree on the lawn near the parking lot. They were dressed in thin T-shirts and shorts, but perspiration shone on their faces, nevertheless. Both were drinking from plastic water bottles. They spotted a boy who was a year older than them a few yards away. He smiled at them and kept walking toward the street.

"There he is, Cory Lauderdale, Mr. Unreachable," Priscilla sighed.

"Big deal," Rosemaria responded.

"Boys like you. Why don't you care?"

"I have other things to think about. My parents expect me to get into college, so I can't think about boys."

"I know all that, but don't you just feel like you'd like to touch him. Stare at his beautiful face for an hour? He already has muscles, unlike most of the pathetic boys around here."

"He's okay." Rosemaria looked up and down the parking lot. "My mom was supposed to be here by now. I hope she didn't forget that we got off early today."

"Maybe she got an audition or something?"

"She usually gets a day's notice on those, and she didn't say anything."

"Has she worked recently?"

"Not since the play closed."

"My mother has a friend who's an actress. I don't think she's even in the union yet."

"My mom's in two unions, but you have to know somebody to get jobs. That's what she says."

"Yeah, my mom too. I'd never go into acting unless I knew somebody important who could hire me."

"It's not a job for my mom—it's her calling. She hates having to do other jobs to earn money," Rosemaria said.

"You want my mom to take you home when she comes? She said she'd be here by two thirty."

"I guess."

"Do you think Cory has a girlfriend? He's always with somebody different."

"I don't give it much thought, Pris."

"Do you still want to be a cop like your dad?"

"Maybe. Or a lawyer. Something where I go to work every day and get paid but it's still interesting."

"Yeah, it has to be interesting—and fun!"

They laughed.

"I think I see your mom's car."

"Yup, that's it. I'll ask her to give you a ride."

Rosemaria nodded. "Okay."

A new, shiny black Camry pulled up to the curb and Mrs. Lovett, blond and pretty like her daughter, leaned down and waved at the girls. Priscilla jumped up, ran to the car, opened the passenger door, and said something to her mother. She looked back at Rosemaria, smiling and waving her over. Rosemaria gave one last look around, realized her mom was not coming, walked to the car, and got in.

* * * *

The robbery-homicide division at the downtown Central Community Police Station was unusually quiet for a Wednesday afternoon. Lyle and Steven were both on their computers, filling out witness reports regarding a homicide that had occurred two weeks before for which they had yet to focus on one viable suspect.

Lyle looked over the top of his computer and saw that Steven, sitting at his desk across from him, was intent on his typing. He used the two-finger system. It took him a while to get the information into the system. "Did you finish the garage guy's report yet?"

After typing in one last sentence, Steven looked up. "Yeah, I'm wondering about the man in the blue jogging outfit who seemed in a big hurry to get gassed up. The way he kept his face turned away from the security camera is a major tell. Forensics got a partial license number and is narrowing down red 1989 Chevys with wrecked back bumpers.

Lyle's phone rang and he picked it up. "Homicide, Sergeant Hirschberg." He listened for a moment. "Hey, Loo, we don't usually handle domestics. Crandall and Harris are on patrol in that area right now. Shouldn't it be their call?" He looked over at Steven and waved his forefinger around in the air, nodding at the receiver. "Okay, we'll take a ride over and see what's going on. If it looks dicey, we'll call in SWAT" He listened and made some notes on a pad "You got it." He hung up, grabbed his Glock out of his drawer, holstered it, and started putting on his jacket that'd been hanging on the back of his chair.

Steven did the same. "What's up? Why us?"

"You know that biker thug Ziggy Shriver who lives on Rosetta Street and who always gets in fights with his biker mama, Lori Lou?"

Steven followed Lyle out the door. "Yeah? Everybody knows he murdered his former partner in those liquor store holdups, but so far Lourdes and Messina haven't been able to pin it on him."

They were rushing down the hall as Steven double-checked his pockets for his gear. He felt a bump in his handkerchief pocket and smiled as he took out a Snicker's bar before tucking it back in—Rosemaria. "So why us?" He asked again as they clambered down the stairs and out the door.

"One of their neighbors called it in. It seems as if this fight is even worse than the ones where they ended up in the front yard—lots of yelling and sounds of furniture falling over."

They got to their car and Lyle opened the trunk. He tossed Steven's vest at him, and they both strapped them on. Domestics could get ugly. Lyle continued, "You're the only guy who's ever been able to talk to that maniac, so they figured you can calm him down the way you did last time." Steven hopped in behind the wheel, with Lyle riding shotgun. Steven pulled out into the street and headed west.

"He was half in the bag when we went there. Remember? He tried to take a swing at me and fell down. All I did was help him over to the couch, and he passed out. Then his wife attacked me with a rolled-up magazine and told me to mind my own freakin' business."

"The woman's almost as big as he is."

"Not quite. He's about six four and two hundred eighty pounds. She's barely five ten."

"And grossly overweight. She's still got some major moves though, according to Messina. When they went by to ask questions after the part-ner was found dead in a gully by the freeway, she landed a fist in Lourdes's chest that knocked him against the wall."

They both sat quietly, staring at the house.

"I'm not looking forward to this," Lyle griped. "Let's wait until the noise stops. Maybe they'll kill each other."

"We should only be so lucky."

* * * *

Rosemaria used her key to unlock the front door and went in the house. "Mom! Mom, are you here?" She put her backpack on the kitchen table and walked down the hall. "Mom?" She opened the door to her parents' bedroom. The bed was made, and everything was in perfect order, as usual.

She walked back to the kitchen, grabbed a can of Coke out of the refrigerator, and started pulling pens, books, and papers out of her backpack and putting them on the table. She made a disgruntled noise with her mouth, opened her notebook, and read the assignment that was due in two days. "My favorite historical figure from the time of the Civil War, but not Abraham Lincoln." She looked up at the ceiling, thought for a moment, and said to herself, "That's easy, Harriet Tubman." She wrote the name in her notebook and opened her history book.

The door from the garage flew open and Olivia walked in, breathless. "I went by the school, but you weren't there!"

"You were late, Mom."

Her mother smiled sheepishly. "I'm sorry. I decided to go by the animal shelter." She disappeared and Rosemaria heard the car door open and close. She came back into the kitchen holding a small, white poodle in her arms. "Her name's Yvette. Isn't she cute?" Her mother put the poodle on the floor, and the dog immediately ran over to Rosemaria, who plopped herself down on the floor. Yvette was overcome with excitement and squirmed into Rosemaria's lap and pawed at her shirt, trying to lick her face.

Olivia was all smiles. "I've been going to the shelter hoping to find a purebred poodle for a long time, and then finally, today, there she was! She's totally potty-trained, so I won't have to worry about doing that. The owner brought her in, so she would have been put down tomorrow. I had no choice but to bring her home."

Rosemaria was captivated and snuggled Yvette in her arms. "She's awfully sweet." She looked up at her mom. "How about food and a bed and all that?

"Oh, I've got that covered—bed, toys, food, all of it." She disappeared into the garage, leaving the door open so she could keep talking. "That little girl won't want for anything, believe me!" She came back in carrying two big shopping bags in one hand and a doggie bed in the other. She dumped them all down on the floor before closing the door. "Whew. I'm all worn out!"

"Is Dad okay with this?" Rosemaria asked, as Yvette burrowed into her arm pit.

Olivia sat on the floor next to Rosemaria. "Of course. I told you both I wanted a dog, but it had to be the right one. Yvette is the right one. I'll put her bed in my bedroom with all of her toys." She stood, grabbed the bed and toys, and carried them down the hall.

Rosemaria looked down at Yvette, who was looking up at her with shining eyes, emitting occasional barks that sounded more like squeaks from a rubber toy. "It looks like I've got myself a new friend."

She called down the hall, "Hey, Mom?"

"What is it, dear?"

"It's my birthday in two weeks. Can I have a party?"

"Sure, honey. Would you bring Yvette in here? I want to see how she likes her new bed."

CHAPTER FOUR

Steven, with Lyle in the passenger seat, navigated through downtown streets in a rundown neighborhood near County Hospital and finally stopped in front of a two-story house with blue paint so badly chipped it was coming off in sheets the size of paper plates, revealing a moldy gray siding underneath. The cement steps were cracked, and black garbage bags were piled up beside the small porch.

The detectives could hear yelling coming from inside the house, both male and female voices. Lori Lou was almost as loud as Ziggy. The front curtains of the house next door moved slightly, and they could make out the face of an elderly black man peering out from behind them. Lyle took out a notepad and handed it to Steven. "We can't just go knock on the door. He could shoot our heads off. Here, why don't you give him a call since you're his pal and all that?"

Steven took the pad and studied the number.

Lyle grinned. "You sure we don't want to wait until this whole thing dies down?"

Steven gave him a look, then took out his flip phone and dialed. He blew air out of his mouth and waited. Nothing. The yelling inside the house stopped. Steven was about to hang up when Ziggy picked up. He was holding a cell phone to his ear as he looked out the window at Steven and Lyle sitting in the unmarked car.

"What do ya want?"

Steven sat up in his seat. "Ziggy! Remember me? Detective Baker. We had a little talk a while back about your partner."

"Never had no partner."

"Neighbors have been complaining about all the commotion in the house. Why don't you let Lori Lou come out on the porch so we can make sure she's all right?"

"She's indisposed."

"That doesn't sound too good, Ziggy. Let us have a look at her."

"Forget it. She doesn't want to come outside."

"Then I'm afraid we're going to have to come inside, Ziggy."

Steven heard Lori Lou screaming in the background, "What are you guys waiting for? He's going to kill me!"

The phone went dead, and Ziggy turned away from the window as the front door started to open. They saw Lori Lou's face in the opening. Before she could step outside, she was yanked back from the doorway by her hair. She screamed and struggled to pull Ziggy's hands away. The door slammed shut. Steven grabbed his radio and reached for the door handle.

"We can't go in there alone," Lyle said.

"We have to. He could seriously hurt her while we sit here and wait."

"The neighbors have called in complaints at least ten times. She never presses charges. She's as nasty as he is."

"What if this is the one time he decides to kill her?"

Lyle hesitated, but Steven was adamant. "She's a bitch on wheels, but we can't let that happen on our watch."

Lyle shrugged. "Let's do it then."

They stepped out of the car and cautiously moved up the walkway to the house, their hands on their weapons. No sound emanated from the house, and there was no movement in the front window. They walked up the two steps and stood on either side of the front door.

"Ziggy." Steven spoke conversationally but loud enough for Ziggy to hear him. "Everything's cool. We just need to make sure that Lori Lou is okay."

A bullet ripped through the front door from inside, and Steven and Lyle dove off the porch and pinned themselves to the side of the house.

Both men were stunned. They pulled out their Glocks. "What the hell?" Lyle managed to choke out. "Has he gone bonkers?"

Steven brought out his radio. "Dispatch, this is Sergeant Baker. We need the SWAT team now at 682 Rosetta! We're pinned down and can't move. Do you copy?"

A voice crackled back, "Copy that, Sergeant. They're on their way."

Steven turned off the radio and whispered to Lyle. "I'm going around back. You stay here."

Lyle nodded. Steven stayed close to the house and ducked under the front window. He moved slowly, hunched over, carefully sidestepping rusting appliances and rotting trash on his way to the backyard. A shot was fired from inside the house and a bullet broke the glass of a window right above him.

Lori Lou, standing near the window, screamed, "So shoot me! Go ahead and shoot me! I don't care anymore!"

An ancient car body with no wheels sat in the yard a few feet from the back door. Steven ran toward it and ducked down behind the car, using it as cover. He trained his weapon on the back door. "I'm not having another suspect take off on me," Steven mumbled to himself. He figured Ziggy's beloved Harley must be in the garage. If he decided to try to escape that way, Lyle would have to shoot him.

After what seemed like an eternity, Steven could hear sirens from several blocks away. The back door flung open, and Ziggy started out the door. Steven fired and Ziggy ran back inside the house.

Steven yelled out. "You're trapped, Ziggy! Give it up! SWAT's on the way!"

Steven could hear the SWAT trucks pull up and the sound of cops running up either side of the house. As he waited behind the car, through the window he could see members of the SWAT team as they cleared the kitchen then broke through the back door. Cautiously, Steven stood up from behind the car. Movement caught his eye and he glanced up to see Ziggy fly out of a second-floor window, slide down the sloped roof, and drop to the ground. He got up, limping.

Three SWAT team members were there in an instant. "On the ground! Hands above your head! Now!" Ziggy bent over as if to lay down and pulled his gun out of his pocket. He took a wild shot just before he was riddled with bullets. Steven felt a sharp pain in his neck. He stumbled forward two steps and dropped to the ground. He looked up at the other cops, who looked back at him, suddenly noticing he'd been hit. Then everything went dark.

*　*　*　*

The more Rosemaria read about Harriet Tubman, the more she admired her—growing up a slave, enduring years of suffering and beatings as a child, then as an adult rescuing seventy slaves and taking them north to freedom. Rosemaria was awestruck as she read of Harriet's exploits working for the Union Army, leading her own troops, and helping liberate over seven hundred more slaves. No one could ever hope to accomplish what Harriet had, but her work as a suffragette and for women's rights was something Rosemaria could identify with. Both of Rosemaria's parents, in their own ways, were high achievers. As she finished reading all the information she had found on the web about Harriet and began to write her paper, she decided then and there that nothing would get in the way of her living a worthwhile life. She loved her friends, but a lot of what they talked about was silly, especially boys. There was so much more to life than that. But meanwhile, she did want to celebrate her birthday with her friends. Everybody was entitled to some fun.

Her thoughts were interrupted by her mom, wearing shorts and a T-shirt, coming in the front door with Yvette, who was pulling on the leash. Olivia unhooked the leash from the collar, and Yvette bounded over to Rosemaria, who scooped her up and accepted wet kisses.

Olivia plopped down on the couch. "Wow, that is good exercise. Yvette loves to run. It's hard to keep up with her."

"I guess you'll have to train her better."

"No, I want her to have fun on her walks. It's her time."

Rosemaria scratched Yvette's tummy as the little dog writhed on her back in ecstasy.

"Mom, I was thinking about who to invite to my party. Are twenty people too many?"

"Twenty is fine," Oliva answered absently. "Yvette must be hungry." She got up from the couch just as the phone rang. "Will you get that?"

Rosemaria put down her pencil and went to the wall phone. "Hello?" She listened for a few seconds and then her body began to tremble. "What?" she screamed. "Mom!"

Olivia saw Rosemaria's stricken face and grabbed the phone. "Yes, this is Mrs. Baker." Olivia slumped down into a kitchen chair. "Is he—is he—?" She couldn't make herself say the words. "Oh, thank God! I'll be there right away." Half-dazed, she stared out the window. "Your father's been shot."

"Will he be all right?"

"They don't know. I have to go to the hospital." She looked around, disoriented. "I'll have to change. You stay with Yvette."

"No! We have to go now, and I'm not staying with Yvette!"

Olivia rubbed her face and tried to regain her equanimity. "All right. I'll put her in the bathroom for now." She picked up Yvette, who had sensed the dark mood change. Olivia headed down the hall with Yvette and called back to her daughter, "Get in the car!"

Rosemaria pulled her sweatshirt out of her backpack and headed for the garage door.

* * * *

Olivia braked to a jarring stop in the parking lot outside the ER of the Good Samaritan Hospital and flew down the walkway to the entrance, with Rosemaria close on her heels. She went inside and approached the nurse sitting behind the desk. Olivia was hyperventilating and could barely get the words out of her mouth. "My husband—Detective Baker. Where is he? I have to see him."

The nurse, who had seen every kind of emergency in her ten years working in a downtown hospital, responded quietly to Olivia's question. "Your husband is in surgery right now. He was shot in the neck and lost a lot of blood before they transported him here."

Olivia was shocked. "In the neck?" She shook her head back and forth. "He won't die, will he? He won't die?"

Rosemaria stood forgotten at Olivia's side, even more terrified than her mother.

"He has two excellent surgeons working on him. What I can tell you right now is that the bullet nicked the outer layer of one of the carotid arteries. There was no spinal injury at all. So, his chances are good. You can wait on the second floor outside the surgery center. Check at the desk. The doctors will be with you as soon as they finish."

"Second floor, second floor. . ." Olivia looked around, unable to focus.

The nurse pointed down the hall. "That way, to the right."

Olivia walked quickly toward the elevators. Rosemaria ran to keep up.

When Olivia and Rosemaria entered the waiting room, they saw that Lyle and Lieutenant Farber, Steven's boss, were already there. Farber, a gruff, stocky, banty rooster of a man who tended to run his fingers through his thick, brown hair when he was agitated, was speaking with several other cops who were milling around, impatiently waiting for word. Lyle shot out of his chair as soon as he saw Olivia and wrapped his arms around her. "He's going to pull through. Don't worry. They have the best surgeons in the world right here." He helped her to a chair and then turned his attention to Rosemaria. "Nothing is going to happen to your dad. He's the toughest guy I know."

Lieutenant Farber joined Lyle in reassuring Olivia and Rosemaria. "He's in the best place he could possibly be. They'll take good care of him." He hesitated awkwardly, then walked toward the desk, asking for an update for the umpteenth time.

Rosemaria, her face stained with dried tears, watched him walk away and saw the receptionist shake her head in response to the Lieutenant's question. She sat down next to her mother and leaned against her. She patted her mother's knee. "Dad would never leave us, Mom. He promised me."

Olivia responded, blinking back tears, "I know, sweetheart. Your dad would never leave us."

The other detectives came over one at a time and offered Olivia brief, encouraging comments, then went back to standing or pacing outside the entrance to the OR. Every time a doctor came out, they all looked up expectantly.

Olivia suddenly started muttering bitterly to herself. "I knew this would happen. There's always more, more, more rotten people to chase after. What's the point?"

Rosemaria took her mom's limp hand in hers. "He likes it, Mom. He really likes his job."

"That's fine for him. What about us?"

Rosemaria took her hand away and clasped her own hands together. She began to whisper under her breath.

Olivia glanced down at her. "What on earth are you doing?"

Rosemaria didn't look up. "I'm praying. Priscilla prays all the time. She says it works."

"I don't know what good that'll do. God never seems to care too much about what I want."

Her mother's hurtful words struck Rosemaria to the depths of her soul. Her mom had a wonderful life with a daughter and husband who loved her. Didn't that mean anything to her?

After several minutes of talking to God, Rosemaria opened her eyes. She saw a doctor wearing surgical scrubs come out of the OR and begin speaking in hushed tones to the cops who gathered around him. Rosemaria hopped out of her chair, and Olivia was not far behind. They forced their way through the crowd of cops and stood in front of the doctor.

"How is my husband?" Olivia asked. "Is he alive?"

The doctor responded calmly. "He came through the surgery just fine. We patched up the ripped artery and gave him plenty of blood to replace what he had lost. He'll be in intensive care for a couple of days, so you won't be able to talk to him. You can see him through the glass, though." He looked at Rosemaria. "He's hooked up to a lot of machines, but don't let that frighten you. They're all doing the job they were meant to do."

Lyle heaved a huge sigh of relief and smiled at Olivia. "What did I tell you? He's too tough to die."

Olivia and Rosemaria found themselves surrounded by cops, all with happy, relieved expressions, sharing well-wishes and prayers for a speedy recovery. *It does work*, Rosemaria thought to herself. *It does work!*

* * * *

The pain hit him with excruciating force. It was concentrated in the left side of his neck, and he felt like he was nailed to a board. All he could see were blurry forms and light coming from one side.

The face of a middle-aged woman appeared a few inches away from his face. "Mr. Baker. Mr. Baker, can you hear me?" She had worry lines etched into her face. "You're in the hospital. You had surgery on your neck but you're going to be fine."

He was in a hospital. Thank God! He could get something to stop the unbearable pain. "Eh… eh," he managed to get out.

"What's that, Mr. Baker?"

"Eh… need…" He tried to say painkiller, but the word wouldn't come out. It took all the effort he had in his body to lift his hand and point to his neck. "Pain…" It came out as a whisper.

She turned away, then came back holding a needle. She used it to inject something into his IV. "It won't be long now. I gave you something that will take away the discomfort."

His eyes cleared and he saw that he was in the bed nearest to the window. The patient next to him was curtained off, but he could hear his moans. He'd always hated hospitals—the smells, the sounds, the wheelchairs, the whole nine yards. And here he was, stuck in one. At least the pain was beginning to let up. He closed his eyes and enjoyed the opioids coursing through his body.

* * * *

Rosemaria's mother was trying to save money on electricity, so the air conditioning was turned off even though it was another stifling spring day. All Rosemaria had the energy to do was lie on her bed and stare up at the ceiling. Today was the second day that they had visited her father, but he still hadn't woken up again since they'd given him pain medicine. The doctor said that was to be expected and that Olivia and Rosemaria should not worry on that account. Easy for him to say—her father was just another patient to him. To Rosemaria, he was the sun, the moon, and the stars, the only father she had. So, until he was wide awake and could talk to her, she would worry.

She forced herself to her feet and looked at the books lying on her desk. She had finished the Harriet Tubman paper and was pretty proud of it, truth be known. She had asked Priscilla to come by to pick it up and then deliver it to their history teacher. Mr. Pulver had given her a few extra days to finish the paper, considering what was going on. But there was some math homework she hadn't done and was dreading doing. She hated math with a passion. She had to concentrate extra hard in class to keep her mind from wondering and focus on getting another A to keep her grade point average up.

She peeked out her window and saw that her mom was still sitting in the lawn chair on the back patio, smoking. Yvette was curled up on her lap.

Ever since the shooting, her mom had been smoking several packs a day with no let up. Nagging her about smoking did no good, so Rosemaria and her dad had both stopped asking her to quit a long time ago. At least she couldn't smoke in the house or car.

Rosemaria was heading back to her desk to work on her math homework when the phone rang. She raced into the kitchen and picked up. "Hello … He did? … Thank you!" She ran to the patio door and screamed at her mom. "Daddy's awake!

* * * *

Euphoria blanketed his senses. He could stay like this forever. Pure bliss. God bless morphine and all its children. He felt a smooth, little hand pick up his, and he opened his eyes to see a perfect face and green eyes smiling back at him from a foot away.

"Hi, Daddy," the little face said. "I brought you something." She took a Snickers bar out of her sweatshirt pocket and laid it on the bedside table. "For later."

A beautiful, grown-up version of the small face appeared. "Hi, honey. The doctors say you're going to be good as new."

He started to speak but his mouth was filled with phlegm. He cleared his throat and whispered. "I must be in heaven to be surrounded by angels."

Rosemaria laughed. "We're real, Daddy." She had steeled herself ahead of time in order to be cheerful. It was hard seeing him lying there so weak and helpless. But she'd rather die than let him see her act like a wuss when he needed her to be strong for him.

"And when you get home, you'll find out we're not angels at all," Olivia said. "We have written orders from the doctor on how you have to behave. You'll be calling us both Nurse Ratched after the first day."

He managed a weak smile. "You're a lot better looking." He felt the warm, comforting glow of whatever the last nurse in the room had injected into his IV starting to drag him under.

His daughter's face was inches away again. "Go to sleep, Daddy. We'll see you when you wake up again."

He felt himself drifting away and didn't have the strength to squeeze the soft, smooth hand that lay gently on his palm.

CHAPTER FIVE

Rick Pulver—amazingly young and good-looking for a history teacher, according to the girls at Garden Grove Elementary School—was waiting for his students to settle down after their lunch break. Unlike when he'd been teaching middle school for three years, wondering why he had chosen the teaching profession, he enjoyed teaching these little kids. They were very young and some of them, like Rosemaria Baker, were incredibly smart. Middle school kids were the worst—completely undisciplined, with unbridled energy and hormones on the verge of raging out of control. Trying to teach them anything was not for the faint of heart. Regretfully, soon the students he was looking at now would be just like them.

He waited for the chatter and laughter to die down and picked up a stack of papers on his desk. "I was pleasantly surprised by the essays you wrote on your favorite Civil War historical figures. Many of you actually went beyond plagiarizing the encyclopedia, researched other sources, and wrote compelling, insightful papers. I gave you this assignment because it can get a little boring and pointless to merely memorize names, dates, and places, and then regurgitate it all on a test. I'm not in favor of that kind of teaching, although, unfortunately, that's what the educational system requires of us these days. So, I choose to risk my neck and push the outer limits of the envelope to actually encourage you all to think for yourselves." A boy in the second row raised his hand. "Yes, Lenny."

"What do you mean 'pushing the outer limits of the envelope'?"

Mr. Pulver waited for a couple of students to stop snickering. "Actually, a good question. Test pilots came up with the expression. It means to go beyond accepted limits of behavior." Then he quickly added, "But in a good way. In other words, have the courage of your convictions, be willing to stand up to criticism, and do what you think is right and take it as far as you can."

Pam Lincoln, a plain girl who wore glasses, sat in the front row, was serious as all get out spoke without raising her hand. "They won't fire you, will they?" She looked worried.

"I hope not. It helps to have friends in high places when you push the outer limits." *Like a father on the board of ed*, he added silently to himself. He began to pass out the papers, walking up and down the aisles, making positive comments as he stopped by each student. "As I told you before, I'm going to ask a couple of you to read your papers aloud to the class." He handed out the last paper to Rosemaria. "We'll start with you, Rosemaria."

She looked up at him. "You mean like now?"

"Yes."

Rosemaria stood up, walked to the front of the class holding her paper, and looked out at her classmates—lots of friendly faces, except for a couple of morons who never paid attention. She had known that reading her paper in front of the class was a possibility, so she had practiced in front of the mirror in her bathroom. She couldn't stand the thought of being boring so, using what acting techniques her mother had shared with her, she had rehearsed her presentation, striving to be understated and yet convey the emotions that Harriet's life generated within her.

She began to read, starting with Harriet's most exciting and daring exploits. Her mother had advised her that you always do that to capture the audience's interest. Then she told them of Harriet's tragic childhood and described in detail how she escaped from her slave owners, then returned south to rescue other slaves—usually in the dead of winter—and eventually became a Union soldier leading her own troops. Rosemaria recounted how Harriet had continued to work for causes she believed in until the day she died, in a rest home surrounded by family and friends.

She finished reading and looked up at her teacher. She thought that she'd done even better in front of the class than she had in her bathroom and hoped Mr. Pulver thought she'd done well, too. She was happy to see that he was smiling.

"I get the clear feeling that you very much admire Harriet. How did reading about her make you feel on a personal level, Rosemaria?"

"Well, it made me want to try to do something important with my life and not just take up space on this planet. I figured I couldn't even come close to doing what she did, but now that I heard you talk about pushing the envelope, even though I can't be like her, I want to push the envelope, too. I just don't know where I'm going to do it yet."

"Are there people in your life who you think do that?"

Rosemaria didn't hesitate. "My dad. He never lets anything stop him when he's going after a criminal."

A look of concern flashed over Mr. Pulver's face. "Is he feeling better?"

"He came home three days ago, and all he can think of is going back to work."

"That's understandable. When you spend every day chasing bad guys like your father does, it's hard to stay home and do nothing. Exceptional work, Rosemaria. You may sit down. Jaime, you're up next."

Rosemaria walked to her seat and acknowledged her friends who were giving her thumbs-ups and high fives. She sat down with a feeling of accomplishment. It felt nice being the center of attention. When she was younger, she'd hated having people look at her, but now it was okay. She thought of her mother onstage for two hours and all those lines she had to memorize. Rosemaria shuddered. She didn't love performing that much. Her mind drifted away from Jaime's lackluster reading of his paper to planning her birthday party, although it was over a week away. Her father and Priscilla's mom always had to organize them because even though her mother meant well and said she'd help, Rosemaria always knew it would be up to her and other people. Her dad had insisted that he was ready for a party and looked forward to being surrounded by a little levity for a change. Her mother was back to concentrating on trying to get auditions, not getting any, and being depressed. Only Yvette seemed of any comfort to her. Oh well, Rosemaria had something to look forward to, and nothing could spoil that. She was going to be ten in a week and a half, and now that her father was going to be healthy, life was good.

* * * *

Close to twenty screaming and laughing nine-and ten-year-old party revelers filled every square inch of the Baker's backyard. The Claytons had brought several folding tables from their church, and Priscilla's mom had put disposable paper tablecloths on all of them. Steven had cooked up batches of chili and had grilled hamburgers on the patio grill so everyone could make up their own burgers with all the trimmings. The cake had been devoured, the birthday song sung, presents opened, and the tables were in disarray, covered with paper plates with remnants of food still on them and half-filled cups of juice. Steven had ordered a huge piñata and had the delivery men hang it from the oak tree in the back. Lonny Hanigan had been the one to finally bash in the poor paper-mache donkey and got the prize of a gift certificate to Chuck E Cheese. All the edible goodies that spilled out had been first come, first serve and everybody scrambled to get theirs.

Rosemaria loved every second of it. Her father was a gracious host to the other parents, who tried to not interfere with the kids having a good time no matter how rambunctious they might be. Even her mother made an effort to enjoy the party and didn't spend as much time inside as she usually did at Rosemaria's birthday parties. Her father had told her that her mother was never comfortable with other parents and felt misunderstood by them because of her profession. In reality, most of them didn't give it a second thought. Her father was used to making up for her mother's reticence in social situations, and Rosemaria could tell he enjoyed the party and watching his daughter have a good time. She suddenly felt the urge to run to him and give him a hug.

"Having fun, Daddy?" She asked, a huge grin on her face.

"You know it, honey. The only positive thing about getting shot is knowing I get to stay at the party all the way through without being called in to work."

"I think people are starting to leave. I'll help clean up."

"You will not! You're the birthday girl. Let the old folks take care of that."

She giggled. "You're not old."

"Older than you. Now, go find your mother and tell her the party's winding down."

Rosemaria went inside and walked down the hall. She knew where she would find her mother—cuddled up with Yvette watching TV in her parents' bedroom. She opened the door and saw that the TV was off and that her mother was lying on the bed, staring up at the ceiling.

"Mom, are you okay?"

Olivia didn't move. "I guess."

"People are leaving. Do you want to say goodbye?"

Her mother seemed listless and uninterested. "You say goodbye for me."

At a loss for words, Rosemaria stood in the doorway for a few seconds, then closed the door. She found her father outside. "Mom doesn't want to say goodbye to anybody."

Her father noticeably stiffened, then breathed deeply and smiled down at his daughter. "Then we'll say goodbye to everyone and thank them for coming. Priscilla's mom and Mrs. Clayton will help me clean up. You can gather up your presents and take them to your room."

"Okay."

"You can't let your mother ruin your birthday, honey. Her depression has nothing to do with you. You know that."

"Don't worry, Daddy, I'm used to it. Nothing can spoil today for me."

Her father, suddenly feeling worn out from all the activity, sat down at a table to take the weight off his feet. "Have I told you how proud I am of you, my daughter?"

"Not lately, so you can tell me again."

"I'm prouder of you than I am of anything else in my life."

"I feel the same way about you, Daddy." And with that, she ran off to say goodbye to Jaime and his mother as they headed toward the side of house and out the gate.

An hour later, after the yard and house had been cleaned up, Rosemaria was taking Yvette for a walk just for a couple of blocks. Her mom had asked her to do it, saying she was tired. Rosemaria was ordered to not go any farther because she was too young. Rosemaria thought that was silly. If any stranger approached her, she knew exactly what to do. She could scream louder than all heck and could run faster than anybody at her school. If she knew karate she could stay and fight, but her dad didn't think that was necessary for her to learn at her age. She didn't try to wheedle him into it because that kind of thing didn't work too well with him, anyway. In a year or two, when she was older, she was sure she could talk him into it.

Rosemaria wished that her mother wouldn't always be so depressed. Sometimes, when her agent called with an audition, she'd be higher than a kite, laughing and talking, so hopeful. Then when she didn't get the part, she'd spend hours sitting alone in the yard, smoking, with Yvette in her lap or at her feet. Rosemaria wondered how her dad could stand it. What kind of a wife was that to have? At least Rosemaria had her father to make up for her mom being so selfish. And she had Priscilla and all her other friends. Yeah, her poor father. He probably regretted ever having met her.

If only her parents could be more like Matt and Carol Clayton. Carol had a normal job at a medical clinic, and Matt was an accountant who worked from home. They weren't beautiful and handsome as her parents, but they always seemed to be so peaceful and happy. She loved that her parents were special and sometimes exciting, but she longed for a little bit of normalcy in her life.

She walked back into the house and heard voices coming from the bedroom. She knew she wasn't supposed to eavesdrop but, like any good detective, she wanted to hear what was going on. Holding a squirming

Yvette close to her chest, she heard her father talking in a tone of voice she had never heard from him before.

"If you can't act like a gracious hostess even at Rosemaria's birthday party, you have a real problem, Olivia. You need to see a psychologist before this gets any worse. You have a daughter for God's sake. You can't put it off any longer." His voice had a sharp edge to it.

Her mother's response was slow, and it sounded like she was drunk, even though she never drank a drop. "I just need the right break, that's all. I know that it won't be long before I get a job, and everything will be fine."

"And if you don't, then what? You're going to keep on like this, ignoring your daughter and me, barely making an effort to cook meals, and sitting in the yard smoking yourself to death?"

"Oh, for Pete's sake. It's not that bad."

"It's that bad. I've been looking up therapists nearby, and I'm making an appointment for you and you're going to go."

Olivia's voice became louder. "You went behind my back looking for shrinks? How dare you do that! If I need to talk to somebody, I'll call them myself."

"That's just the thing, Olivia, you won't call."

Olivia suddenly began yelling. "Stop trying to micromanage me! I'll do whatever I want! You're never here for me. You're off chasing criminals and don't have time to pay attention to me!"

"One of us has to make a living," her father said cruelly. "And it certainly is not going to be you."

"Bastard!" Olivia screamed at him. "I wish I'd never met you!"

"I'd say the same, but then Rosemaria wouldn't exist and that would be a tragedy."

Rosemaria scurried away from the door, but not before Yvette dropped to the floor and bounded into the bedroom. She jumped on her parents' bed while Rosemaria waited a few seconds before entering, pretending she'd just gotten there. "We had a really good walk, just up and down the sidewalk like you said, Mom, I didn't go far."

Her mother grabbed Yvette and held her close, ignoring Rosemaria.

Her father took his daughter's hand, leading her out of the room and closing the door behind them. "You heard that didn't you?"

"Some of it." Then she hurried to reassure her father. "But it doesn't matter. I know she's sick in her mind. I don't hold it against her."

"You're just ten years old. You deserve better than this."

"I don't feel one bit sorry for me. I feel sorry for Mommy. She has so much and can't even appreciate it."

"You had a great birthday, though, didn't you? I think everybody had a wonderful time."

Rosemaria felt tears welling up in her eyes, threatening to spill down her face. "It was, Dad. Priscilla said it was the best ever." She knew she'd better leave before the waterworks began. "I'm going to shoot some hoops."

She hurried down the hall to her bedroom, unable to stop the tears. She grabbed her basketball out of the closet, pulled on a sweatshirt, and ran out the front door to the driveway. Her dad had hung the basket over the garage door at regulation height like she'd wanted, and the free throw line had been painted in relation to the basket according to professional measurements. To do otherwise would have been unthinkable. She had stopped throwing free throws underhanded this past year. Her goal was to become proficient by the time she reached her full height. She aimed and the ball hit the backboard. She tried again and missed by a mile. The tears had stopped flowing, but snot was running down to her mouth from her nose. She wiped it off with the sleeve of her sweatshirt.

She knew that the key to dealing with her mother was to focus on things that were in her control. It was up to her how well she played and how good her grades were in school. Ever since she could remember, she had tried to make her mom happy, and knew it was a lost cause.

Suddenly, the unfairness of it all overwhelmed her. She ran around to the far side of the garage and leaned up against the wall as the dam broke and she began to cry in earnest. She deserved to have a mom who was normal like the other moms! Why did hers have to care more about her dog and whether she got acting jobs. It wasn't fair. Rosemaria wasn't a whiner and faithfully did all her chores. What had she done that was awful enough to deserve this?

After a few minutes, she wiped more tears and snot on her sweatshirt and shook off the self-pity. She walked back to the free throw line and concentrated. She threw. Swish. Threw again. Backboard. More backboard. Swish. She gave every bit of her attention to her throws. The sniffling stopped. She was back on track.

CHAPTER SIX

heers and whistles erupted in the robbery-homicide squad room as Steven walked through the door without his arm sling. He laughed in surprise and embarrassment. "Stop! All I did was get shot. I didn't even arrest anybody."

Lyle stood up from behind his desk and walked over to give him a brief man hug and a gentle pat on the back. "Glad you're back, buddy. The criminal element has raged out of control while you were gone."

Steven acknowledged the continued attention of his fellow detectives with a shake of his head and sat down at his desk opposite Lyle's. Farber came out of his office, a big smile on his face.

"I could say that Ziggy turned out to be a bigger pain in the neck than you thought, but I won't because you might throw your stapler at me."

Steve grimaced. "Your pitiful joke is more painful than the bullet."

"Well, no worries about Ziggy. He got aired out with about twenty bullets. He's about as dead as anybody can get."

"Everybody cleared?"

"For shooting a dirtbag who was trying to murder a cop? You bet. No problems there."

"How about Lori Lou?"

"We took her in and questioned her, but she refused to say anything about anybody. She said if we kept her there, she'd lawyer up. She's in the wind now. Probably found herself another biker to treat her like crap."

"Probably." Steven pasted as pleasant a look as he could muster in the direction of Farber. "You know, Lieutenant, I'm perfectly fine now. I'm ready for more than desk duty. I can handle being out in the field when the need arises."

"You're riding a desk for the next week, no ands, ifs, or buts. Doctor's orders. No amount of complaining will do you any good."

Looking only slightly defeated, Steven said, "Okay, I'll go through the cases we have and see what I can do."

"Sounds like a plan, big guy."

Lyle had been paying close attention. "I could use your help on the human smuggling case. We're still nowhere with that. The FBI came in to 'help' us"—he made quote marks in the air—"but with them it's all take and no give."

Steven shrugged. "Big surprise. I'll check for updates from the last couple of weeks if there's any. What are you working on?"

"The Sam Clemente murder. It looks like it was personal, might have something to do with Clemente maybe fooling around with Jack Sandusky's wife. But Sandusky has an airtight alibi, and we haven't found any leads to lead us to the hitter. Helmsley and I are going to talk to Sandusky again and see what we can shake loose about his dealings with Clemente."

"I'd like to be there."

"I hear ya, but we need to get on this before it gets ice-cold."

"I'll be here feeling sorry for myself should you need me."

Lyle took his Glock out of his desk drawer and grabbed his jacket off the back of his chair. "If I had a wife as beautiful as yours, I'd never leave home."

Steven watched him stop briefly at Sergeant Helmsley's desk, and then the two of them went out. *If only beauty were everything*, he thought. Then he started up his computer.

* * * *

The casting office was located on the 20th Century Fox lot, which was now a mere shell of what it had been during its heyday, when little Shirly Temple had saved the studio from going under. *Oh, to have been here back then*, Olivia thought as she drove down Century Boulevard. But she reveled in the possibility that today she actually had a chance to become one of the fortunate actors who worked in the hallowed soundstages of the Fox studios.

The parking structure was adjacent to the studio, and Olivia had no problem finding her way to the office building where casting for the TV show *LA Undercover* was taking place. She had dressed simply, tied back her hair, and gone easy on the makeup, wanting to look as plain as possible. This was not a glamour-girl role. She would be reading for the guest starring role of a cop who goes undercover, is exposed, and then murdered. Her first guest starring role! If she booked this part, it could be the first of many. She signed in and took a chair, eyeing the other actresses who were all studying their sides. She decided to go out into the hallway where she could whisper her lines aloud before being called in. She had easily memorized her lines and had used everything she'd ever learned in acting class to prepare for this audition. She had gotten inside the character's skin and knew what made her tick. She'd never felt so right for anything. She only had to wait half an hour before she heard her name called. She went through the door with a smile and displayed the supreme confidence only a stage actress possessed. She said her brief hellos to the casting director and her assistant behind the camera. Then the camera was turned on and focused on her and the casting director said the magic words, "Whenever you're ready."

In the scene, she is being questioned and tortured by a group of drug dealers whose gang she had infiltrated. At first, she is offended that they would even suspect her of being a cop, then she gradually becomes more and more fearful until she breaks down in tears and begs them to spare her life. Olivia moved through the transitions effortlessly, and when the climax came so did her tears. She had nailed it.

The casting director handed her a tissue and allowed Olivia to calm her emotions. Then she asked Olivia if she could wait outside for a few minutes. Olivia nodded. "Of course."

Olivia was shaking as she went back to the reception area. She had just done the best audition of her life. She'd left nothing on the table. She sat down and didn't look at the other actresses still waiting to read. No one went in or out of the casting director's office. Finally, the door opened, and the assistant approached her and whispered, "We'd like to put you on hold for three days. If that's agreeable to you, we'll call your agent and let him know."

Olivia nodded and projected a calm she did not feel. She almost stumbled to the outside exit, and then she sat heavily on a bench by the door. On hold! That meant she had a very good shot at getting the role! They wanted to show her tape to the director and producers who would make the final decision. If anybody read better than she did she would be shocked. She stood up and walked back to her car. She sat behind the steering wheel and decided to follow Rosemaria's example. She prayed like she had never prayed before, which was pretty much never. Rosemaria said it worked, and if it did, Olivia wanted to cover all her bases. *Dear God in heaven, let this be it. Let this finally be it.*

* * * *

Rosemaria and her father sat at the dinner table, astonished at Olivia's cheerful bustling about the kitchen as she prepared to serve her first home-cooked meal in over a week. Using potholders to protect her hands from being burned, she set a big, glass pan down in the middle of the table with a dramatic flourish. "I made lasagna for us today. Totally from scratch." She laughed. "It's about the only thing I'm capable of making that tastes good." She looked at her husband and daughter. "So, dig in and tell me you like it." She handed Steven a big serving spatula, while Rosemaria waited her turn.

Steven took the spatula and dug himself out a huge piece. "I was wondering what was going on in here today. You kept both of us out of the kitchen for two hours. But the wonderful aroma gave us a hint as to what you were up to." He picked up a bite with his fork, waited for it to cool, and put it in his mouth. He looked at Olivia, who was observing him anxiously. "Mmm, absolutely delicious."

"Really? You like it?"

"You've outdone yourself."

By now Rosemaria had served herself a big portion of lasagna as well. She blew on it before taking a bite. She chewed appreciatively and nodded at her mom with her mouthful. "Yeah, Mom. This is the best ever."

Oliva sat down to serve herself. "And don't forget to eat your salads. That's the healthy part."

Steven put another big forkful in his mouth and waited until he swallowed to ask, "Call me crazy, but I think something must have happened to put you in a mood like this."

Oliva put her fork down and rubbed her hands together nervously. "Well, I didn't tell you, but I had an audition today for a guest starring role on *LA Undercover*."

Rosemaria's mouth fell open. "Really? Wow! That's incredible. Did you do okay? When will you know if you got it?"

"Well, it looks good for me because they placed me on hold for three days."

Steven looked puzzled. "They put you on hold? What does that mean?"

"It means that the casting director thought I was really good, and she needs to show the tape to the director and producers, then they make up their minds who they want. When they put you on hold it means you can't go on auditions or take other jobs because then you won't be available for their show."

"So, you have to wait three whole days to find out?" Rosemaria asked.

Steven jumped in. "I'm proud of you, hon, and we'll keep good thoughts, but you know you can't count on these things."

Rosemaria hoped her mother wouldn't fly off the handle at hearing that.

Olivia didn't let his comment spoil her mood. "Don't worry, I'm not saying I have it in the bag, but being on hold is the next step to booking the part. This would be my first guest starring role, separate card and everything."

Rosemaria didn't know what that meant but it made her mom happy. "I'll pray for you, Mama, really hard, every day."

"Oh, would you?" She reached out and took her daughter's hand. "I'm happy you have faith in me even if certain other people don't."

"I didn't mean—" Steven began, but Olivia laughed it off.

"It's okay. After all the times I've lost out, it's normal to think this is just one more time I'll go down in flames. But it isn't. I feel that. I nailed this one and my time has come."

They all dug into their lasagna as Rosemaria and her father exchanged worried looks.

* * * *

The robbery-homicide squad room was almost deserted except for Steven and Sergeant Messina typing on their keyboards. Steven was trolling through arrest records looking for any connection between Sam Clemente and Jack Sandusky. Sandusky swore up and down that he'd nothing to do with Sam besides hanging out in a few of the same bars, and that his wife Helen's dirty weekend with Sam in Carmel was meaningless. Besides which, he and his wife hadn't been getting along for more than two years and were in the process of getting a divorce.

Clemente had been in the construction business like Sandusky. Occasionally, they'd bid on the same project, but Clemente had not been in the same league as Sandusky, whose company had built some fairly large office buildings downtown and elsewhere. Clemente had been relegated to public school add-ons and two-and three-story medical clinics. So where was the connection? Finding out about the wife's cheating had to have been the tipping point after something a lot bigger had happened.

He had barely started looking into possible criminal history of both men and their families when his phone rang.

It was Rosemaria. "Hi, Daddy." She said she was in the principal's office, using her landline.

Steven sat straight up. "What is it, honey? Is something wrong?"

"I don't know. Mom didn't pick me up again, and Priscilla wasn't in school today, so I didn't have a ride home."

"Where are you now?"

"In the principal's office. The bus left already."

Swearing under his breath, Steven grabbed his coat and said to Messina on his way out, "Tell Hirschberg I had to pick up my daughter. I'll be back in a couple of hours."

He ran out the door and jumped in his car. He wove through downtown traffic, hopped on the freeway, and headed toward Simi. He grumbled under his breath, "Where the hell is she?"

Rosemaria was sitting in the principal's office reading when her father came in. She jumped up and stuffed her book into her backpack while her dad gave his apologies to the principal for having to keep her after hours. They walked to the car, and Rosemaria seemed more excited than put out. "Can I go with you to the station, Daddy? I'd like to see where you work."

"I think we better go home and see what your mother has been up to don't you think? Maybe something's wrong. I haven't been able to reach her."

"Okay." She was disappointed.

"We'll do it soon, kiddo. I promise."

He pulled into the driveway, and Rosemaria used her key to open the front door. Steven followed, and both walked down the hallway to the bedroom. There was no sign of Olivia.

Steven picked up the receiver on the kitchen wall and dialed his office. "Yeah, Messina, tell Lyle that I have a bit of an emergency at home. I'll see him tomorrow... Yeah, thanks." He hung up and looked at his daughter, who had sat down at the table and was chewing on her fingernails. "I'm sure she's okay, sweetheart. You know how she is about losing track of time."

"I guess so."

"I'll call the hospitals nearby and see if she's been taken to the ER."

"No! Don't do that yet. I'm sure nothing's wrong."

"Don't you think it's best to find out right away?"

"No. I don't want to know." Rosemaria's lower lip was quivering. "She's just late, that's all."

"All right, I'll tell you what. I'll fix you a sandwich, and then if she still isn't home, we'll call."

While Rosemaria was eating her sandwich, Steven went into the bedroom and used the landline to call the squad room. Lyle picked up. "Could you do something for me?" Steven asked him.

"Sure. What's wrong? Is it Olivia?"

"I don't know. She's not home, and I haven't been able to reach her. Can you check for any accident reports anywhere in the LA area?"

"You bet. You want to hang on, or should I call you back?"

"You can call me back."

"Done."

Steven hung up the phone and sank down onto the bed. What the hell was his wife up to now?

Rosemaria came in, holding her peanut butter and jelly sandwich. "You didn't have to do it in secret."

"I'm sorry. You're right. Lyle will call me back if there's anything to report."

"I'm not a baby you know."

"I forget that sometimes. I'm sorry."

The phone rang and Steven grabbed the receiver. "Yes?" He looked at his daughter as he listened. "Okay, thanks, Lyle." He hung up. "She hasn't been in an accident. Looks like we'll just have to wait."

It was dark by the time they saw the lights of Olivia's car pulling into the driveway. They were both seated at the dinner table as she walked in from the garage, holding Yvette. She seemed startled to see them both staring at her. She put Yvette on the floor, who immediately ran over and began pawing at Rosemaria's legs. "What? What are you looking at me like that for?"

Her lack of remorse enraged Steven, but he had to hold it together for Rosemaria's sake. "You want to tell us where you've been and why you didn't call us?"

Olivia shrugged off her jacket and hung it on the rack by the door. "You'd think that you would have a little more consideration after what I've been through."

"And what is that exactly?"

"I decided to go for a drive because I was getting tense waiting for the casting director to call. So, I drove past Santa Barbara and then turned around, thinking I'd take a walk on the beach. I got lost trying to get there and ran out of gas on a dirt road and then had to walk for at least a mile to find a gas station."

"And you didn't call because…?"

Rosemaria sat, her hands folded in her lap, ignoring Yvette at her feet, staring at her mother without saying a word.

By this time, Olivia was pacing in and out of the kitchen area. "Well, you can stop interrogating me like I'm one of your criminals."

"Because…?"

"*Because* it wasn't that late yet, and I thought I could make it back in time to pick up Rosemaria."

"And then what?"

"I got gas, drove to the beach. I took a walk with Yvette that was longer than I meant to walk. By the time I got on the freeway, there had been a terrible accident, and I've been sitting on the 101 ever since. By then, my cell phone battery had run down, so I couldn't call." She looked at the two of them and curled her lip in disgust. "You'd think I'd get some support and sympathy from my own family. But I guess that's too much to ask." She headed down the hall to the bedroom.

Rosemaria and Steven were still at the kitchen table when Olivia, with Yvette running to keep up, opened the sliding door and went out to the patio. They saw the glow of her cigarette in the dark and briefly caught a glimpse of the cold, angry set of her mouth.

* * * *

"I think I may have found something on the Clemente killing." Steven was at his desk in the robbery-homicide squad room. He'd been forced to set aside his worries about Olivia's emotional problems to concentrate on work.

Lyle looked up from his computer. "Lay it on me. I've hit a wall with the Duran disappearance. I feel like I'm going around in circles."

"So, ten years ago Clemente and Sandusky were in about the same place with their construction companies—neither one of them doing that great but both up-and-comers. Then they both bid, along with some other companies, on a huge warehouse project down in San Pedro for Layton Industries. Ten blocks worth of construction. Sandusky got the job and made a fortune on it, while Clemente did only fair to middling projects, then had a few rough years before rebounding."

"How does this relate to the murder of Clemente? Sounds like he was the one who had a good reason to hate Sandusky and kill him."

"After Sandusky won the bid, Clemente hired investigators to find out if Sandusky had received some inside information. Apparently, Sandusky attended USC with somebody at Layton. Clemente sued. The lawsuit didn't go anywhere, but the two men hated each other's guts."

"I know you're leading me toward a big climax right now."

"Not so big. But get this. After Clemente's wife died of cancer three years ago, Sandusky's wife, Helen, who had been friends with Clemente's wife, began an affair with him, according to witness statements. It wasn't just one weekend in Carmel. What I'm thinking is that Helen was not only getting cozy with Clemente but was sharing some ugly secrets about her husband's business practices, which according to people in the construction business have always been a little shady."

"The wife refused to talk to us."

"That's because she was going through a divorce and didn't want to rock the boat until it was a done deal. In two weeks, they sign the final decree. I think she might be willing to talk then."

"Sandusky has an alibi for the time of the murder," Lyle pointed out.

"He hired somebody. Come on, the reports say that Clemente was checking on a possible construction site at midnight on a Tuesday, and some homeless person shot him and robbed him. Give me a break."

"That's from an anonymous source."

"Yeah, like Sandusky."

"So, let's wait two weeks and see what the wife has to say. She's probably scared to death she'll be next if she talks."

"We'll put her in witness protection."

"We'd better nail her down before she heads to Vegas looking for boy toys to spend Sandusky's money on."

"Lots of those right here in LA."

"Then let's hope she sticks close to home."

CHAPTER SEVEN

The school auditorium was filled with the excited voices of twenty-five fifth and sixth graders as they walked to their places on the risers on stage. Rosemaria, being one of the tallest in her class, stood in the back, while Priscilla, one of the shorter students, was in the very front.

"Okay, everybody. Let's settle down." Mrs. Betz, everybody's favorite teacher, walked down the center aisle of the auditorium with a big smile on her face. She was in her early twenties and, according to anybody's standards, was very beautiful with short blond hair and a perfect figure. "We're just going to go through some of the basic instructions for our program today to make sure we're all on the same page."

She reached into a cardboard box that was sitting on a chair and took out a handful of audiocassettes and began handing them out. "These are tapes of the two songs we'll be singing. I gave you the sheet music already but singing along with the tape will help you learn your parts. They're labeled either alto or soprano so make sure you get the right one."

The very thought of having to sing made Rosemaria's blood run cold. She couldn't carry a tune if you paid her with a boxful of Snickers bars.

Mrs. Betz noticed the expression on Rosemaria's face and chuckled. "There may be some people here who think they can't sing. That is not true. Who's heard of Christopher Plummer and Katharine Hepburn?"

Nobody raised their hand except Rosemaria. Mrs. Betz acknowledged her with a nod. "Who were they, Rosemaria?"

"They're famous actors. He was in *The Sound of Music* and she was in movies since before my mother was born."

"Exactly. Both of these famous actors sang in musicals. Christopher Plummer did not have a classically trained singing voice, but he half sang, half talked his songs in *The Sound of Music*, and it worked! Katharine Hepburn sang in a Broadway musical and did the same thing. The reason it worked was because they had such passion and verve that no one cared that they didn't sound like trained singers."

Connor, a boy standing in the front row, raised his hand. "What's verve?" he asked and there were a few smirks from people who didn't know what it meant either.

"Rosemaria, do you know?"

"Verve is when you're completely involved and committed to the material and give all your energy to the role."

"That's what your mom does when she's acting, right?"

"Yes."

"So being able to stay completely on pitch does not matter. If we give it our all, the audience will react to that." Mrs. Betz turned to one of the African American girls standing in the front row. "Besides, Alisha, along with singing the solos, will sing the chorus with everybody else. You can follow her lead and not worry at all what you sound like. Just have fun!"

Alisha, standing next to Rosemaria, smiled confidently. She already knew where her future would lead.

"At our next rehearsal, in two days, I'll have your 'Just Say No' T-shirts and will hand them out to you. But don't wear them until the performance in two weeks. Does anybody have any questions?" Nobody did. "Okay, then. Let's do our best to make Nancy Reagan proud!"

Connor raised his hand again. "Who's Nancy Reagan?"

Some of the kids laughed, and others rolled their eyes.

"Now, now, there is no such thing as a stupid question. Nancy Reagan was the first lady when her husband, Ronald Reagan, was president. She started the 'Just Say No' campaign to encourage kids not to take drugs. And schools everywhere have programs to support her efforts."

The door to the auditorium opened, and Rosemaria saw her mother walk in and take a seat in the back. Oh God! Now what? She still had hours left in school. What was her mother doing here? Mrs. Betz dismissed the group, and Rosemaria ignored Priscilla who was waiting to walk out with her. Her mother stood but didn't approach Mrs. Betz. She just waited by the door until Rosemaria reached her.

"Why are you here? Is something wrong?"

"I'm taking you home now."

"But I still have classes."

"I have to be home all afternoon because my agent is going to call and let me know if I got the part."

"Can't you just take the call on your cell?"

"No. Whatever happens, good or bad, I want to be home, not out driving around."

"And for that I have to miss school?"

"Don't get smart with me, young lady. Let's get your things out of your locker and go."

With a heavy heart, Rosemaria did as she was told.

* * * *

All the lights in the house were out when Steven came home at 11:30 at night. He had been on a stakeout for hours. He hadn't been cleared by department medical personnel for normal duty yet, but at least he could sit in a car and surveil with the best of them. He walked from the garage into the kitchen and saw the familiar glow of Olivia's cigarette out on the patio. He walked down the hallway and opened Rosemaria's door to make sure she was asleep, then he went back to the kitchen and carefully slid open the patio door.

He spoke quietly. "You're still up?"

"You could have called."

"I was on a stakeout. I couldn't."

"Today was important for me."

He braced himself for an outburst. "You didn't get it."

She threw her cigarette in the ashtray and leaned over, keening as if in terrible pain.

"Gosh, I'm sorry, honey." He touched her shoulder and she jerked away as if touched by a burning poker.

"Leave me alone! You've never understood how much this means to me! Now all my hopes for a breakthrough role are gone! I'll never have a chance like this again!"

"You can't say that. You're still young."

"I'm not young. To them, I'm old. It's over for me!"

As her voice became louder, Steven looked around, hoping the neighbors had their windows closed. "You need to calm down. You're taking this way too hard."

"I suppose you think there's something wrong with me. That I need professional help?"

"Come inside. We can talk about that tomorrow."

"No! We're never going to talk about it. I don't care about anything, anymore. My life is over. I always told myself that I'd rather be dead than fail as an actress, and now I've failed. There's nothing left for me!"

"You have Rosemaria and me. Isn't that something?"

She stared at him, hard and cruel. "You've never understood me. Never. Leave me alone."

"Olivia, just come inside—" He put his hand on her arm, but she flung it aside, whispering viciously.

"Leave me alone. Do you hear me? Leave me alone."

Steven backed away and slipped inside the house. He was sure the neighbors must have heard some of that, but he hoped Rosemaria was still sound asleep. He opened her bedroom door and saw that she was. Thank God. He would have to deal with this in the morning and try to convince his wife that she needed therapy. Their lives couldn't go on like this.

After her father closed the door, Rosemaria opened her eyes and stared up at the ceiling. She knew that she needed to compartmentalize her mother's insanity and live her own life, separate from her. She had a normal father who loved her and that would have to be enough.

* * * *

Rosemaria and Priscilla were seated at a picnic table in the school courtyard munching their peanut butter and jelly sandwiches, surrounded by their classmates also eating their lunches and enjoying a respite from the drudgery of classes. "Is your dad coming tonight?" Priscilla asked.

"Yes, he said for sure, no matter what."

"I can't wait for my parents to see how good we are. Mrs. Betz says we're very professional the way we behave on stage."

"And I think we sound good too. Of course, Alisha helps drown out any bad singers like me."

Priscilla laughed. "You always exaggerate how bad you sing. But you say your lines better than anybody, that's for sure."

"From now on, I'll be taking the bus to and from school. My mom can't do it anymore."

"Too bad she's so depressed. Maybe she'll get over it in a while."

"I don't think so. She doesn't care about anything."

"Well, you just have to decide that's a grown-up problem and let your dad handle it."

Rosemaria smiled at her friend. "That's just what I'm going to do. Want to run lines again?"

Priscilla groaned. "Don't you ever get tired of practicing?"

"You start."

Priscilla sighed and began her recitation.

* * * *

Rosemaria looked at herself in her bathroom mirror. Her dad always told her how pretty she looked, and sometimes she almost believed him. She was wearing her green "Just Say No" T-shirt, which brought out her eyes and went well with her auburn hair, and she liked what she saw. She was going to have fun tonight and sing her heart out like Mrs. Betz had told them to do. She would make her dad and Mrs. Betz proud.

Rosemaria could smell the cigarette smoke from her parents' room. Her mother had started smoking in the bedroom the day after she didn't get the role in the TV show. She didn't give a crap that her husband said secondhand smoke was bad for their daughter. He couldn't stand the smell of it and now slept in the spare room. Rosemaria barely spoke to her mother anymore except to be polite and say good morning and good night. Her mother didn't care one way or the other if Rosemaria completely ignored her.

She wasn't going to let any of that spoil her evening. Priscilla and her parents were picking her up, and her dad would drive straight to the school. He had called an hour ago and told her nothing short of a terrorist attack could stop him from coming.

Rosemaria was opening her closet door to take out her jacket when she heard a quiet thump come from down the hall. She stopped short and listened but heard nothing else. She decided she had imagined the noise and put her jacket on, picked up her backpack, and walked out into the living room to wait. But her conscience bothered her. What if something was wrong with her mother? She better check or she'd think about it all evening. Suddenly feeling apprehensive, she walked slowly down the hall to her parents' room. She opened the door and saw her mother lying on her stomach on the floor, near the bathroom. Yvette was crouched beside her, whimpering, and pawing at Olivia's arm. Rosemaria rushed to her mother's side and knelt down, forcing Yvette to move away. Yvette barked two pitiful barks that sounded more like anguished cries.

"Mom! Are you all right?! Mom!" Rosemaria tried to roll her mother onto her back, but she could barely get her to stay on her side. Her mother's eyes were halfway open and blank as if the light inside them had gone out. "Mom!" She shook her mother's shoulder, hoping she would open her eyes all the way and tell Rosemaria she was okay. She rubbed her mother's hand and touched her face, willing her to blink her eyes and breathe, all to no avail. But she refused to accept that her mother was gone. Doing what she had been trained to do by her dad, Rosemaria scrambled to her feet and stumbled over to the landline phone that sat on the bedside table. Her fingers were shaking so hard she could barely dial 911.

"This is Rosemaria Baker at 411 Rosewood Drive in Simi Valley. Please come right away! My mother is on the floor and not moving!… No, I don't know CPR! Please, just hurry!

She hung up and swallowed the bad taste in her mouth that was rising from her stomach. She knew that what she had to do next was call her father and tell him that he needed to come home right away. But she didn't want to! Out of nowhere, self-pity overwhelmed her. *This wasn't fair! She was only ten years old! Why was this happening to her?* Her fingers were poised to dial but her mind refused to remember her father's office telephone number, even though she knew it as well as her own. She shook her head to push away the cobwebs in her mind that were tangling up the numbers, but they still wouldn't line up in the right order. She glanced sideways at her mother, who hadn't moved and was still frozen, lying on her side as Rosemaria had positioned her.

The awful truth was unavoidable. She had to face it. Her mother was gone. How could Rosemaria tell her father that? Why did she have to be the one to break his heart? She sank down to the floor, her back resting against the side of the bed, still grasping the receiver. For the first time in her life, Rosemaria's memory failed her. All she could do was stare at her mother and wait for the ambulance to come.

* * * *

After the funeral, Rosemaria couldn't bear talking to people and accepting their kind gestures of sympathy. She sat alone on a bench in a far corner of the backyard, where sounds of muted conversation floated out the sliding door from inside the house. Her father had told her that her mother had died of some complicated word having to do with her heart and heavy smoking, but she knew that wasn't completely true. She had died because she hadn't wanted to live anymore. To her mother, life wasn't worth living because she had failed, and because having a husband and daughter who loved her hadn't been enough.

It had taken all of Rosemaria's willpower not to scream when she saw her mother's casket sitting over the grave. The very thought of such a beautiful person being lowered into the ground and covered with dirt filled her with such horror that she had to fight the urge to succumb to hysterics. She had felt her father's hand on her shoulder and became determined to not let him down by making a scene. She'd looked up and seen that his eyes were closed, and his face was pulled tight, making no effort to hide his grief. She bit her lip and let the tears flow. She had wanted to be strong for her father, but her heart was broken too, just like his. At that moment, it had been too hard to be strong, even for her.

Later, when everyone was gone, she would change her clothes, go outside, and shoot some baskets. That never failed to help her focus and forget. She was all her father had now, and she wouldn't let him down.

CHAPTER EIGHT

EIGHT YEARS LATER

The passing years had been kind to Steven. He was as fit and trim as ever, though his hair revealed a lot of silver threading through the brown. He was on the phone with Rosemaria in the squad room when Lyle came in and slapped a copy of the *LA Times* on his desk. "Remember her?"

Steven glanced at the front-page picture and held up his forefinger. "Gotta go, kiddo. Do well on the exam. See you on Saturday." He hung up and studied the picture of Helen Sandusky, just as beautiful as she had been eight years ago.

Lyle, his red hair almost gone and carrying a few extra pounds around his midriff, hung his coat on the back of his chair. "How's UCLA treating your daughter? Still all work and no play as always?"

Steven answered absently, "Yeah, nose to the grindstone." He read the article that accompanied the picture of Helen Sandusky. "She's come up in the world. Marrying a state senator. I wonder if she'd still be too scared to testify against her ex-husband?"

"Anything she knows or ever knew is hidden deeper than Jimmy Hoffa's cement covered corpse. Her new husband may be able to protect her, but she's not digging up that dirt again. It's not good politics." Lyle paused, then said, "Speaking of politics—Farber's being promoted to captain, and the word is one of us is in line for his job."

Steven shook his head. "You're welcome to it. I'm not getting tied to a desk issuing orders. If I can't be out on the streets investigating, I'm not a cop anymore—I'm a den mother."

"Just askin' in case they come to me and beg."

"I'll celebrate mightily if you want it and get it. No hard feelings, believe me."

"Good to know."

Steven went back to the newspaper article. "Sandusky got away with murder and we all know it. It pisses me off that we couldn't touch that sleazeball. Now he's richer than God and acts like he's citizen of the year."

"Somebody talking about Sandusky?" Farber was walking in their direction. The lines in his face had deepened and his formerly thick hair had thinned to the point that he was now paying a lot of attention to hair-transplant commercials.

Steven held up the paper. "We were just reading about his ex-wife marrying Senator Worthington."

"Ah yes, the woman of many secrets." Farber held up the paper and scowled. "She could have helped solve that case for us. She'll never talk now."

He laid the paper back down on the desk. "I got a call from on high that I'm supposed to send somebody to check out the old Camden office building on 3rd Street that's just been sold to a developer. The owner is worried that people are breaking in and stealing fixtures before he gets bids on the contract to turn the place into lofts or condos or whatever they call crappy apartments in depressed areas. He wants somebody to check it out."

"Why are you telling us this?" Lyle asked. "That's for patrol."

"Don't worry, I'm not sending the two of you. I know you've got more important things on your plate. The thing is Sandusky is one of the people putting in a bid on the remodel contract."

"I'm sure everything he does now is on the up and up, especially when it comes to a rinky-dink job like this," Steven offered.

"Crooks sometimes just can't help themselves, ya know." Farber gave a backward wave on his way to his office.

"Why would Sandusky be willing to do a small-time job like that?" Lyle mused. "Doesn't make sense." He shrugged. "Let's go to lunch. I didn't have any breakfast."

Steven grabbed his jacket. "Now that Rosemaria is living in the dorms, I never bother with breakfast anymore."

"There's a stack of pancakes in our future."

"Let's do it."

* * * *

Rosemaria, completely unaware of the beautiful young woman she had become and brushing off compliments as irrelevant, sat impatiently at her desk, waiting for the period to be over. She had finished her exam in record time. The questions had been so easy that she'd almost fluffed a couple of answers by not paying close enough attention. She was sure she'd aced it. Political science was her favorite course; trigonometry her least favorite. Actually, she hated it, but in order to graduate with honors she had to do well.

Her roommate had dropped out of school after four weeks, and it was heaven having the whole dorm room to herself with no distractions. She could study as much as she wanted with no one playing annoying music or talking nonsense about their boyfriends. She made time for workouts at the gym, jogging around the campus, and shooting hoops with friends but that was about it for amusements. She usually saw her dad on Saturdays. They would have dinner; he would ask about school, and she would ask him about work. Life was pretty boring at the moment, but that was okay. Her real life wouldn't start until after she graduated, and she decided what the heck she wanted to do with her life. Law school or the police academy? Plenty of time to figure that out.

Fifteen more minutes to go until the end of class. She grimaced, dug her trig book out of her backpack, and proceeded to force some of the material into a brain that just did not care.

* * * *

Steven pulled into his driveway, exhausted. He and Lyle had been interviewing potential witnesses in a fatal hit-and-run, but no one had seen a thing. A couple of obvious liars had been pulled in and questioned at the precinct to no avail. No one, not even people who had been standing near the point of impact had noticed anything unusual. One elderly lady said she saw a blue sedan speeding down her block as she was walking home from the store and then noticed a body lying in the middle of the street. But that's all she saw. When it came to gang-related hits, people still didn't want to get involved. It had been a cliché for a long time but a reality, nonetheless.

Every time Steven walked into the house, he felt the absence of Rosemaria. She had been such a strong presence in his everyday life. After Olivia died, his daughter had always seemed more concerned about his wellbeing than about herself. Although only ten years old at the time, she seemed to have separated herself from her mother long before Olivia died from coronary thrombosis. Rosemaria had given up, turned the corner, and had become emotionally unavailable to everyone but him. When he had told her that Carol Clayton had a friend who was willing to adopt Yvette, Rosemaria had immediately agreed. He knew she cared for Yvette, but it seemed she wanted nothing to do with anything that reminded her of her mother.

He opened the refrigerator door and grabbed a bottle of beer off the shelf and then sank into his easy chair in the living room. He couldn't help being worried about his daughter. She had no social life and was oblivious to the affect her beauty had on men. She went out on a date every once in a while, but any attempt on the young man's part to turn the relationship into anything meaningful was doomed to fail. She was focused on her schoolwork. And Steven had no intention of interfering in her personal life. He was in no position to offer advice. He had gone out with maybe a total of five women since Oliva had died, but none of them came close to evoking the strong feelings he had for Olivia. His work and his daughter were all he needed to be happy. Why invite an unknown variable into his life that could cause problems? He was content to keep things exactly as they were.

He was startled to hear the landline ring. Few people used the number, except for Rosemaria when she couldn't get him at the office or on his cell. He dragged himself up from his chair and into the kitchen to pick up the receiver. "Yes, Sergeant Baker here."

He heard a quivering, whispering voice. "Sergeant Baker, this is Helen Worthington."

For a moment he was taken aback. Had he heard correctly? "Helen Worthington?"

"Yes. Used to be Helen Sandusky. You investigated my husband for the murder of Sam Clemente."

"How did you get this number?"

"It was on your card you gave me years ago. I kept it."

The shock of hearing her voice wore off. "Why are you calling me now, eight years later? It would have been extremely helpful if you'd talked to us then."

"I'm sorry. Can you meet with me tonight?"

That surprised him. "Tonight?"

"Yes. It's urgent that I talk to you."

"Where are you wanting to meet?"

"I'll come to where you are. There's a restaurant called Hal's in Simi. No cameras cover the parking lot. I drive a black Lexus. We can talk in the car."

"All right. What time?"

"In one hour." She hung up.

* * * *

Steven saw Helen's car in the far corner of Hal's parking lot as soon as he drove in. There were still plenty of diners who had their cars parked in the lot. She must have felt safe knowing she would not be alone at some deserted rendezvous point. He parked a few spaces away from her car and, after looking around for anything that seemed the least bit suspicious, he got out of his car and walked toward hers. He heard the click of the passenger-side lock and got in. He couldn't help noticing that she was even more attractive in person than her photograph in the paper.

Steven held out his hand. "I'm Sergeant Baker. To what do I owe the pleasure of this meeting, Mrs. Worthington?" He said, not a little sarcastically.

She shook his hand and held it briefly as she looked him in the eyes. "I'm sorry. I really am." She turned away from him and peered into the darkness, as if looking for unseen dangers. "I know I should have talked to you back then, but I was scared. He had already murdered Sam. I couldn't say or do anything that would risk my life."

Steven looked down and shook his head in disgust, forcing air out through his mouth. "So, you knew he killed your friend and yet you've let him walk around free until now. I ask again—why are you here talking to me?"

"I don't want to sit in this car any longer than I have to, so I'll get to the point. I married Jack when I was eighteen, was miserable with him for six years. After Sam's wife died and he and I fell in love, I was finally happy. But Sam was certain that Jack had used illegal means to win bids over him and other contractors. No matter how hard I tried to get him to forget about it, he wouldn't let it go. As you know, he sued Jack but could never compile enough hard evidence, so the lawsuit went nowhere. Finally, I told him I could get access to Jack's laptop and would see what I could find. I didn't expect to hit the motherload, but I did. Jack discovered that someone had been going through his records and assumed it'd been me. I had already printed out plenty of incriminating evidence. Jack found it in the trunk of my car before I could take it to Sam. Sam ended up dead, and Jack told me I would end up the same way if I didn't keep quiet about what I'd found out."

"And that's why you refused to talk to us. I don't know what you expect me to do now."

"Jack has no idea that I made copies of everything I printed out and stored them in a safety deposit box."

"Even if you give that evidence to us, proving that Jack is unethical still doesn't prove he's a murderer. And he would know where we got the information and could still come after you."

"You don't understand! Everything's changed now!"

"So, explain it to me."

"After the divorce, I went a little crazy. I was still young. I'd lost the love of my life and didn't know what to do with myself. I had a lot of money and decided to enjoy myself."

"And you went a little wild, doing things you regret."

"A lot wild—men, drugs, out of control parties, used and abused by strangers I picked up in bars. I think back on it now and it makes me sick. One morning, I woke up in a crappy motel and all my cash and credit cards were gone, and that was it. I cleaned up my act, got a job as a receptionist at a public relations firm, met Joe Worthington who was one of their clients, we hit it off, and then, wedding bells."

Steven rubbed his eyes. "I've had a long day, Mrs. Worthington. I'm happy your life story turned out so well, but I fail to see where I fit into it." He reached for the door handle.

"No! Don't leave! Everything's changed. Jack is desperate for money, and he intends to blackmail me with some pretty brutal pictures if I don't give him four hundred thousand dollars! He obviously had someone following me back then in case he needed insurance to use against me."

"What are you talking about? Sandusky is one of the richest men in town. Why would he be desperate for money?"

"He's heavily in debt to some people he got in bed with years ago. He's so arrogant that he thought he could ignore them. It's all off the books. But now these gangsters—Russian or Ukrainian or something like that—want every penny he owes them. But until he gets paid for his next job, he needs cash to see him through."

"How do you know all this?"

"I still have friends in the company, and the rest I figured out from the documents I have."

"And you want to expose him now or keep hiding all of this from your new husband?"

"I wanted to keep my husband from finding out, but I don't know if that's possible anymore. The people who are after Jack are scary, and he's just as scary. I feel trapped. That's why I came to you."

* * * *

When Rosemaria walked into the robbery-homicide squad room she gave a wave to a couple of her dad's coworkers whom she had known for years and then sat down at his desk. Sergeant Messina was still just as attractive, in a tall, good-looking Italian kind of way, as he had been when her dad used to let her hang around the squad room growing up.

He was on his way out but stopped to say hello. "Have you decided yet if you're going to the academy when you graduate?"

"Law school is still a possibility, but I haven't made up my mind yet."

"You wouldn't be thinking of becoming a defense attorney and going over to the dark side?" he teased.

She feigned shock and horror. "Never! Perish the thought!"

He laughed and went out the door.

She could see through the glass door of Farber's office that her dad and Lyle were having an intense discussion with their boss. She'd hoped to talk him into having lunch with her since she happened to be downtown anyway. Not much could induce her to face the brutal traffic between Westwood and his office, but as part of an assignment from her political science professor, she'd had an interview in a nearby office with a feisty, African American state representative who loved to talk to students.

She intended to ask her dad to take her to Vincente's for lunch. After listening to Representative Marie Collins talk for two hours nonstop, she thought she deserved an expensive reward. Her dad had turned off his computer but logging onto it was no problem for her. His password had been her birthdate since the day she was born. She needed to check her email to see if exam grades had been posted yet. Nothing. She logged off and waited.

* * * *

Farber paced in front of his desk as Steven and Lyle sat facing him. "So now she's supposed to deliver four hundred thousand dollars to a so far undisclosed location. He has pictures of her various indiscretions and she's going to tell him she still has evidence against him, so they're at a stalemate. She wants us to be there at the delivery point so we can grab whoever comes to pick up the money and arrest him, connect him to Sandusky, and then what? It gets us no closer to proving Sandusky murdered Clemente."

"True," Steven admitted. "But we can't arrest whoever shows up. We don't have evidence of wrongdoing on their part, and we don't want Sandusky to know we're going after him. I figure we give her protection when she hands over the money to Sandusky's guy and let him have it. In return, she gives us all the evidence regarding Sandusky's illegal dealings with foreign mob guys. We'll take our time investigating every scrap of paper she gives us and nail down the evidence that Sandusky had a motive to kill Clemente. Helen will testify that he admitted to killing Sam and then threatened to kill her. She's using her own money for the payoff but will spill everything to her husband when we're ready to arrest Sandusky and she can get the senator's people to protect her."

Farber stopped pacing and scratched his head with both hands. "So, when is this delivery supposed to take place?"

"Tomorrow night, but she doesn't know where yet," Lyle said. "Sandusky told her not to bring anyone with her."

"Which she won't," Steven added. "As soon as she gives us the meet-up place, Lyle and I will hotfoot it over there, park a few blocks away, and find a place to set up to make sure the handoff goes down without a hitch. Hopefully, he won't change the location at the last minute.

Lyle spoke up. "I have my son's bar mitzvah tomorrow night."

"Okay then, Baker, you and Messina get surveillance duty." Farber looked at Steven. "Are you up for this?"

"Absolutely."

Steven and Lyle stood up and looked at their boss, who had sunk into his chair with a heavy sigh.

"Better late than never, I guess." Farber said, which produced smiles all around.

Steven was surprised to find Rosemaria greeting him as he walked to his desk. "What are you doing here, daughter? Aren't you supposed to be in class?"

"Hi kid, good to see you." Lyle grabbed his jacket. "I have to go to bar mitzvah practice. See you guys later." And off he rushed.

Father and daughter gave each other a brief hug. "I had to interview Representative Collins for my class and after listening to that woman expound on practically everything that's happening in this city, state, and country, I decided I needed a nice lunch with my dad as a reward."

"I thought you loved politics."

"Political science, yes; politicians, not so much."

"Okay, I can give you an hour. Where do you want to go?"

"Vincente's."

Steven pretended to use his desk to steady himself. "Vincente's?"

"Yes."

"Okay. I'll just forgo paying my electricity bill this month. But we only live once, right?"

"I can't believe I didn't have to resort to whining to get you to agree. Things must be going good in the crook-catching business."

Steven waggled his eyebrows. "Not bad. Things are definitely looking up." He took her arm and ushered her out the door.

* * * *

The meet-up with Sandusky's guy would take place south of Vernon, in the parking lot of an abandoned warehouse. After Helen called Steven and told him the time and place, Steven and Messina immediately drove to the location and parked several blocks away, crossing their fingers that they wouldn't get a call from Helen saying she was to meet whoever somewhere else. They spied a crumbling building across the street from the warehouse that would make a perfect vantage point. Steven got out of the driver's side of the car, carrying a special long-range camera that could record in the dark. Messina took his Smith & Wesson rifle out of the trunk, and they hurried toward the building, staying off the sidewalk, creeping quietly between abandoned dumpsters and broken-down machinery. They walked up cement stairs to the second floor and peered out a hole in the wall where a window used to be.

The warehouse was lit only by nearby streetlights. It was surrounded by ancient chain link fencing with the gate hanging half off. They waited quietly for two hours until they saw a car—an old Ford sedan—pull into the warehouse parking lot at 12:30 a.m., half an hour before the meet-up. The engine and lights turned off. Two people were in the front seats. Sandusky probably wasn't one of them. Steven made sure the camera recorded the car and license plate.

Steven had given Helen no-nonsense instructions. "All you have to do is give the bag to whoever shows up and then leave. That's all he asked you to do. Don't talk. Avoid looking the person in the face and do not walk close to their car. Just turn around and go. Understood?" She had nodded yes, and he hoped she would follow directions.

At 12:55, they saw Helen's Lexus pull into the warehouse lot. Messina aimed his rifle in case something went sideways, and Steven again turned on the camera to record the handoff.

They could see that Helen looked frightened but determined as she opened the door, holding the bag with the money. She walked slowly toward the other car where the two people were now standing by its open doors. They were both wearing hoodies that kept their faces in shadow. Steven and Messina watched her stop several feet away from the other car. One of the men walked toward her and took the bag. She turned to go but something he said stopped her. She hesitated.

"No, no, no!" Steven whispered. "Get out of there!"

They watched as Helen started following the two men, who were now walking toward the door of the warehouse.

"What the hell is she doing?" Messina shook his head in frustration.

Helen disappeared inside.

"Shit!" Steven said.

"What do we do?" Messina asked.

Steven waited for a moment. "We didn't need this confrontation now! What could have convinced her to go inside?"

Messina looked ready to spring. "We can't stay out here. Let's go."

They left the camera and rifle on the cement floor and walked quickly down the steps and across the parking lot to the warehouse door. It was locked.

"Damn!" Steven was getting frantic.

They both peered through the dusty windows but could see nothing. Inside was completely dark.

They looked at each other. "Do we wait for backup or what?" Messina asked.

Steven shook his head and clicked on his radio. "This is Baker and Messina at 298 E. 52nd Street. Need assistance ASAP. Copy?" The operator answered. "Copy that. Units on the way."

They took out their Glocks, exchanged a brief glance, and then Steven gave a quick nod. He shot the lock and slowly opened the door. He indicated for Messina to go left, that he would go right. Their eyes grew accustomed to the partial light, and they could see that the place was filled with piles of broken-down packing boxes and rusted construction equipment.

A shot rang out and a bullet exploded the side of the wooden box a few inches from Steven's head. He ducked down and moved around the corner. Messina had disappeared from his view. He heard movement behind him.

A hard object was smashed into the side of his head, and he fell to the ground, out.

As he regained partial consciousness, Steven felt himself being dragged across the floor, then outside and lifted into the trunk of a car. The trunk slammed shut. Messina was lying next to him and was out cold but still breathing. He heard the distant sound of sirens, which grew fainter as the car moved away from the warehouse. He had no idea in which direction they were headed.

He made the decision that when his abductors opened the trunk, he wouldn't try to fight them. He was too weak and groggy to do any damage. Maybe they didn't intend to kill them, just dump them somewhere.

After about five minutes of what felt like freeway driving, then a few minutes more on surface streets, the car stopped, and the trunk was opened. Steven feigned unconsciousness. Messina was lifted out of the trunk, footsteps crunched over gravel, and then there was a shot and the thud of something heavy hitting the ground. He made his body go limp and hoped they wouldn't shoot him, because there wasn't a damn thing he could do about it if they did. Rough hands dragged him out of the trunk and laid him down on the ground. He could feel the cold air of an open pit a few inches away from his face. Someone took a shot at him just before a foot kicked him over the side. The bullet went into his shoulder, and he steeled himself not to shout on the way down. He landed heavily on top of Messina and wondered if this is where he would die.

CHAPTER NINE

The warehouse parking lot was ablaze with swirling cop lights. Ten or more police cars were jammed into the lot, with two ambulances and the CSI unit parked near the door to the warehouse. Farber was speaking into his cell phone, madder than hell. "Pick up Sandusky now! And hold him till I get back to the station! I don't care how much he squawks! He's not getting away this time!"

Lyle pulled in as far as he could, jumped out of his car, and ran toward Farber. "What happened? How'd they get them out of here so fast?"

"Who knows? Can't find any blood stains. No sign of Helen Worthington."

"I doubt you'll get anything out of Sandusky, no matter how hard you squeeze."

"We found their camera and rifle in the building across from the parking lot. Baker filmed two men at the handoff, but their faces were covered and unrecognizable. We're tracking down the owner of the car." Farber paced back and forth, pulling his fingers through his hair. "This was supposed to be easy. I should've sent more men. I really screwed up."

"No street cameras here I guess?" Lyle asked as he looked around.

"We'll check."

"I should've been with him."

Farber wasn't listening. "I'll make Sandusky talk if it's the last thing I do."

"Don't worry. You'll have lots of help."

* * * *

Rosemaria was sound asleep when the sound of her cell phone ringing penetrated a strange dream about being in front of her poli-sci class and giving a presentation on pesto sauce. She licked her lips and still tasted the garlic from the lasagna she'd had at Vincente's the day before. She checked the time on her phone. It was three thirty.

"Yes, hello. This is Rosemaria."

"Rosemaria, it's Lieutenant Farber." He sounded grim.

Rosemaria bolted straight up as if she had been shot from a cannon. "What's happened to my dad?!"

"I won't kid you—it's bad."

"Tell me!"

"He went to what should have been to a simple handoff last night, but he, Messina, and the woman they were protecting have disappeared."

Rosemaria fell back on her bed. "Disappeared?" she whispered.

"Your dad had a camera, and we got a clear picture of the license plate number. The two men were wearing hoodies so we can't get facial recognition off the video."

"Did you track down who owns the car?"

"We're on it, Rosemaria. There's nothing you can do. We have a BOLO out on the car, and we'll do our best to track him down."

"And when you find him?"

"We'll bring him in and get him to talk."

"Why was my father there? Who are these people?"

"You know I can't tell you that. Let us do our job, Rosemaria. I promise you; we'll find your father."

"By then he might be dead."

"Goodbye, Rosemaria. I'll call you as soon as we know anything."

She hung up and sat on the bed, letting what Farber had told her sink in and contemplating her choices. She breathed in and out heavily for several minutes and made her decision. She pulled on jeans and a sweatshirt, grabbed her purse, and ran out into the early morning darkness.

* * * *

Farber clicked off his phone in frustration and watched as the last of the cop cars left the warehouse parking lot. Forensics would still be there for a while longer, determined to find something to give them a lead on what had happened. He hated giving the bad news to Baker's daughter. Now he had to tell Messina's wife the same thing. His phone rang, and he clicked back on. He listened for a moment then started running to his car and yelled at Lyle to follow him. "Helen Worthington was picked up on the side of the freeway! She's in the ER, barely alive!" He got in his car and sat in the driver's seat, Lyle jumped in to ride shotgun, and they sped lights and siren toward Good Samaritan Hospital.

* * * *

Rosemaria breezed past reception—a familiar face and the daughter of a cop in trouble. She looked around for a couple of seconds to make sure no one was in the squad room and then sat at her father's desk. She figured she better work fast before anybody showed up. She knew forensics would have loaded the footage from her father's camera into the police database by now. She typed in the password and hunted around for where the video might be stored. God knows she wasn't much of a computer expert, but she'd watched her father work on his department computer plenty of times. Finally, she found the video with the right date and time. She watched the video intently as the two men drove up to the warehouse and stopped. She got a good look at the license plate number. She quickly wrote it down. She kept watching as a black Lexus drove into the parking lot and a woman stepped out and walked up to two men standing by their car. She handed one of them a duffel bag, started to leave, but then turned back around and followed the two men into the warehouse. The video ended there.

She logged off the computer and looked through the few folders her father had on his desk. Nothing. In his top drawer, he had the folded front page of a recent *LA Times* reporting that the former Helen Sandusky had married Senator Worthington. Sandusky? She remembered that name from years ago. Her dad had been investigating a murder having to do with somebody named Sandusky. And this dark-haired woman in the picture looked very much like the woman in the video. It had to be her. Rosemaria was starting to put the pieces together. She looked up the phone number of the DMV and, using the phone on her father's desk, she dialed.

"Yes, I need you to look up the name and address of someone with this license plate number. This is Baker in downtown robbery-homicide. You can call me back here at my desk to verify…Thank you. The number is"—she read the license plate number from her notes—"Could you also please fax me a copy of the driver's license of the owner of this car?" She scrolled through her cell phone and found the number that she had used faxing papers to her father more than once. The person at the DMV was happy to comply.

* * * *

Rosemaria, forcing herself to follow the speed limit, wound her way through mild freeway traffic to her house in Simi Valley. The sun was coming up over the mountains. Time was flying by. She quickly unlocked the front door and raced to her room. She tore off her jeans and sweatshirt and changed into the one business suit she owned. Next, she slipped into her black flats as she opened her dresser drawer and pulled out her black, one-piece ski outfit, which she had worn exactly once when a date had talked her into going with him to Mammoth Mountain to ski. Being a very solicitous type, he had bought her a woolen ski cap when they got up there because of snowstorm warnings. That would come in very handy now. It covered her entire face except for her nose, mouth, and eyes. She would cover her eyes with her sunglasses. She ran into the spare bedroom that was now her father's office, pulled back his chair, flipped up the rug, and loosened a couple of floorboards to reveal a small safe. She used her birthdate as the code to open it up and took out her father's Beretta and suppressor. She wished she had gone to the target range with him more often, but at least she knew how to use it. She shut the safe, put back the floorboards, rug, and chair and was tempted to get the rest of the supplies she needed from the garage. But her father might notice they were gone and figure out what she had done if, God willing, he survived his ordeal. Before leaving her phone in her desk drawer, she used it to look for a beauty supply store near Santa Clarita. She stuffed her jeans, sweatshirt, ski clothes, tennis shoes, gun and suppressor into a backpack and checked her wallet to make sure she had enough cash to buy what she needed. She hurried out to her car, drove a few blocks, and stopped at a gas station beside a clothes donation box. She looked around for cameras aimed in her direction and, seeing none, grabbed a skirt that had to be at least a size 13 and a bulky cable-knit sweater. After digging around in the box for a few minutes, she found the prize she was looking for—a huge straw hat. She still needed a burner phone, dark make up, and surgical gloves. She would have to wait until stores opened to find those.

As she headed for Santa Clarita, she prayed that the address the DMV had given her for Sidney Robbins, the owner of the car, was accurate and that he was the person she was looking for. After reaching Santa Clarita, she drove through a middleclass neighborhood until she saw a house for sale. She stopped next to the sign, took a couple of the realtor's cards from the clear plastic box attached to the post, and tucked them into her purse. She was halfway to her goal.

* * * *

Helen Worthington was in stable condition in a private room in the Good Samaritan Hospital. She had a broken leg and a sprained wrist and was covered in bruises. Her face had several lacerations, and her eyes were almost swollen shut. Senator Worthington was sitting in a chair next to the head of her bed, overcome with concern and confusion. He looked up at Farber and Lyle, who were standing at the foot of the bed staring down at the battered, comatose body of his wife. There was no trace of the slick politician on his face or in his demeanor. He was just a man in love with his wife and who was worried sick. The questions came fast and furious. "Why did this happen? Who threw her out of the car? Was it an attempted kidnapping?"

Farber was in the unfortunate position of being reluctant to reveal facts about Helen that she had wanted to explain to her husband in her own way in good time. Now, he wondered how much to tell Senator Worthington that wouldn't put a strain on their marriage. He decided to tell him just enough to satisfy his curiosity. "Your wife had a meeting with some people who worked for her ex-husband."

The senator was appalled. "You knew about this meeting?!"

"I'm sorry, I can't tell you anything more. Two of our detectives who were there to oversee the meet-up have disappeared, and I have to follow leads to find them. I was hoping your wife would be able to tell us something, but since she's unable to talk right now, we have to go back to the station to interrogate someone who might be connected to this."

The senator shot to his feet. "I'm coming with you! I want to know if you're going to talk to that scumbag Sandusky. Is that who you're going to question?"

Lyle had already moved to the doorway, and Farber was impatient to leave. "Senator, don't you think you need to stay with your wife? You can't be of any help to us, only a hindrance. Please, let us do our job."

Worthington turned away and sunk back down in his chair, suddenly drained of anger, all his energy dissipated. "Sorry. You're right, I can't leave her. Will you keep me undated? I'd appreciate it."

"Absolutely. You can depend on it." Farber joined Lyle, passed the senator's men guarding the door, and headed down the hall at a brisk pace.

* * * *

Rosemaria drove to the address in Santa Clarita that the DMV had given her, and, to her relief, there were several cop cars parked outside the house where Sidney Robbins apparently lived. Obviously, she had come to the right place. She parked several blocks away and was happy to see there were no street cameras in the neighborhood. For several minutes, she watched detectives going in and out of houses two blocks in either direction of the Robbin's house. She glanced at her watch and figured the stores where she could buy the rest of her supplies would be open by now. As she drove away, she noticed two detectives coming out of the Robbins house looking disappointed and grim. In all probability, they had not gotten the information they had hoped to find.

She drove back to the freeway, got on, and then took the second exit. She spotted the beauty supply store she had been looking for in a strip mall next to a supermarket. She parked on the far end of the lot, where there were no cameras. She took off her black jacket and changed into the huge skirt and cable-knit sweater that she'd found in the donation box. She planted the straw hat on her head, satisfied that it would completely hide her face from any cameras, got out of the car, and headed for the beauty supply store. She was pleased to see that they had everything she needed—dark makeup, a black wig, surgical gloves, and even a pair of huge sunglasses. She was able to buy a burner phone and a large, glass bottle of Perrier at the supermarket next door. She used her burner to find the nearest Target store. Fortunately, there was one close by. Still wearing her bulky clothes and straw hat, she shopped for a small knife, lighter fluid, duct tape, and medium-width rope. Back in the car, she transformed herself into a deeply tanned, raven-haired businesswoman wearing a slightly rumpled black suit and large, dark sunglasses.

She headed back to Sidney Robbins's house and saw that the cop cars were gone. She parked several blocks away and walked to a house three doors down from the Robbins house. How did a loser like Sidney, who was hired out to kidnap people, manage to live in a fairly nice house in a decent, middle-class neighborhood? She rang the doorbell, flashed her real estate card at the middle-aged woman who opened the door and said as sweetly as she could muster, "Hello, my name is Patricia Lansky. I'm a new realtor and I'm going house to house in case anyone in the neighborhood might be interested in selling."

The woman studied her face, and Rosemaria was afraid she could see right past her phony story and the caked-on dark makeup. "Actually, it's kind of funny you stopped by. We have been thinking of putting our house on the market. Why don't you leave your card and I'll talk to my husband? We might call you."

"Sorry, this is my last card. Any reason you want to move? It seems like a nice neighborhood."

The woman started to close the door. "Let's just say the neighborhood is not what it used to be."

"Well, thank—" The door closed before Rosemaria could say another word. She desperately needed to find a talker. Her father always said talkers were like a Christmas surprise for detectives. You just asked a question, stood back, and let them talk. Sometimes they actually gave up very useful information.

Fifteen minutes later, Rosemaria had introduced herself to five more neighbors, but no one wanted to sell their house or had anything useful to say about the Robbins, no matter how much Rosemaria hinted and cajoled. She decided to try her best bet—the house right across the street from the Robbins.

As soon as the woman opened the door, Rosemaria knew she'd hit the jackpot. The slightly overweight, gray-haired lady who looked to be in her seventies greeted her with a big smile. "Hello, young lady. What can I do for you?"

Rosemaria gave her a great big friendly smile right back, held up her real estate card, gave her Patricia's name and told her she was just starting out in real estate and doing some cold calling. She had heard that there might be some possible sellers in the area and was hoping she could find someone who might want to use her services, possibly the people who lived across the street.

"Well, I know I don't want to sell my house. I love this neighborhood." She lowered her voice, "Until today, that is."

"What happened today, Mrs.—?" Rosemaria asked in all innocence.

"Morgenstern. Maybe you better come in and have some tea, Patricia, and I'll tell you what's going on. You might want to look elsewhere for clients."

Mrs. Morgenstern welcomed her into the house and invited her to sit on the sofa next to the coffee table. "I'll be just a minute."

Rosemaria had to force herself to calm down and not hurry Mrs. Morgenstern. She knew her dad could be lying somewhere, dead or dying, and time was of the essence. *Patience, patience*, she told herself. Something she was not very good at.

Mrs. Morgenstern bustled back into the living room with a tray holding a teapot and two cups. She took her time pouring, while Rosemaria was ready to jump out of her skin. She took a good look at Rosemaria and said, "Is there some reason why you have to wear sunglasses indoors, dear?"

Rosemaria offered her ready-made answer. "Well, I had LASIK surgery two weeks ago and my eyes are still really sensitive."

Mrs. Morgenstern clucked in sympathy. "My sister had that five years ago and said the surgery was a little painful but that it was so wonderful to be able to see after years of being blind as a bat without her glasses."

"Yes, it is amazing what they can do these days." Rosemaria looked expectantly at Mrs. Morgenstern. "So, as I said, one of the houses I was told might be available is the one right across the street from yours. Do you think they might be wanting to sell?"

Mrs. Morgenstern curled her mouth in an expression of distaste and said darkly, "Oh, those people."

"Those people?"

"Who knows what they will or won't do. They never talk to anybody."

"The quiet type."

"I'd be quiet too if I had a son like theirs."

"What's wrong with him?"

"Sidney. Sidney Robbins. A real deadbeat. Never had a job as far as any of us can see. His parents run some rides at Magic Mountain. They're out of work half the time. My friend Eunice says they have to take other jobs to pay the bills. Now their son is on the lam. Turns out he may have killed somebody."

Rosemaria feigned shock. "Did the police arrest him?"

"No, the little creep took off, and nobody knows where he is. We had police asking everybody questions for hours. Why would we know where he's gone? Ridiculous. What a waste of time. They should be chasing down his car like they do on police shows. He's probably halfway to Mexico by now."

"Exactly. And now he's going to get away." Rosemaria was hugely disappointed. She'd been sure Mrs. Morgenstern would know something. She debated whether she should leave and try someone else, but luckily Mrs. Morgenstern wasn't finished.

"They act like they're so much better than the black people who live up the street. Racists, that's what they are. Which is really funny."

"Why?"

"Well, my friend Eunice said that the Robbins leave for weeks in the spring and summer and only come home on weekends. And when they come home, my mailman and the next-door neighbors—the only people who go near them—say they smell to high heaven of garlic. Can you believe it?"

"Does that have a special meaning?"

"Of course. Anybody who carries a heavy garlic smell like that is probably picking garlic in Gilroy. I found out for sure when I crossed the street to go to Eunice's house and saw one of the Fillmore company boxes in the Robbins's garbage out by the street for pickup. They keep it a secret because they don't want anybody to know they work in Gilroy with all the Mexicans."

"You're sure?"

"Yeah. My nephew went up to pick last year but decided it wasn't for him. He saw them coming out of their run-down trailer where all the pickers live."

"Did he tell anybody besides you?"

"No way. We kept that to ourselves. We don't want any trouble from those people."

"You think they might hurt you?"

"As I said, dear, they are a very strange, secretive couple. And now it turns out their son could be a murderer." She shivered. "I don't want him coming after me."

"I totally agree, Mrs. Morgenstern. You can't be too careful when it comes to strange neighbors."

"I didn't even tell Eunice. I don't want her spreading any gossip and have it come back to me. She tends to talk too much."

"Not even the police?"

Mrs. Morgenstern recoiled. "And have them go back to the Robbins and tell them I was gossiping about them? No, thank you! I know how to mind my own business."

Rosemaria almost choked on that last statement. "I think you're absolutely right. And thank you so much—you've been very helpful." She grabbed her purse and stood up. "You don't have to see me out, Mrs. Morgenstern. I need to get back to the office. I'm already really late."

She sailed out the door and walked quickly to her car. She felt it in her bones that Sidney was hiding out in that trailer. Why not? The Robbins assumed no one knew about their guilty secret. They never considered that nosy neighbors who had nothing better to do than involve themselves in other people's business could figure out exactly where Sidney was and not even know it.

* * * *

The stinging pain in Steven's shoulder and his right leg brought him back to consciousness. He could see that Messina had been shot in the chest and was dead. Steven had pressed his handkerchief into his shoulder wound and held it there before passing out. It looked as if the bullet had passed through and the bleeding had stopped, but he didn't dare move for fear it would start up again. They had taken his cell phone, but his flashlight was still in his jacket pocket. If he heard anyone approach, he would turn on the light and yell. For now, he would save his energy. The throbbing pain in his leg was unbearable. Undoubtedly, it was broken. He felt in his other jacket pocket, and a slight smile broke through the pain. Rosemaria had snuck a Snickers bar into his pocket. He managed to unwrap it and took a bite. He would have to make it last until they found him.

* * * *

The 5 freeway wasn't crowded, so Rosemaria floored the gas pedal and was cruising at eighty miles an hour before long. The trip to Gilroy would take at least four hours. She didn't have one minute to spare. Then common sense took over, and she slowed down. If she were stopped and ticketed, the police would find out later where she had been headed. Even if her plan were successful, she would be in a lot of trouble. God forbid they should find the Beretta in the glove compartment. She kept the speedometer at seventy, wishing with every fiber of her being that she could race to Gilroy at one hundred miles an hour.

* * * *

By the time Farber and Lyle made it to the police station, Sandusky had lawyered up, and Farber knew that trying to talk to him was pointless. He had a squad room full of cops who wanted to beat the truth out of Sandusky, just like overly enthusiastic cops got away with back in the day, but that was out of the question. Meanwhile, every law enforcement agency in Southern California was looking for the perpetrator's car. Farber figured he had gone to ground somewhere and was not about to be driving around in plain sight. Every detective in the room was on the computer trying to find something that connected Sidney Robbins to Sandusky. So far, no luck.

Lyle poked his head in Farber's office doorway. "Hospital called. Helen's awake."

Farber grabbed his jacket and ran.

* * * *

With every minute that went by, Rosemaria grew more nervous and tense. She could have told the police where she suspected Robbins was hiding, but it was doubtful they could make him talk. They would haul him in, pepper him with questions, maybe even threaten him. He would ask for a lawyer and that would be that. No, she had to do this her way if her father were to have any chance of being found. She couldn't figure out how her father, Messina, and the Sandusky woman had just disappeared like that. It didn't make any sense. But all she wanted was to find her father. The cops could figure out the rest.

* * * *

Farber and Lyle made it to the hospital in record time and raced down the hall to Helen's room. The two cops showed their IDs to the guards and went inside. Helen still looked like death warmed over, but they could see that her eyes were moving back and forth through the slits between her swollen lids. She offered a weak smile when she saw them.

Farber pulled up a chair and sat while Lyle stood next to the senator near the window. It was obvious from the resentful expression on Senator Worthington's face that he was not happy with the dangerous situation the police had put her in.

"I hear you're ready to talk," Farber said to Helen.

Helen whispered, "You'll have to lean closer. I can't talk very loud."

Farber did as she asked. "What happened, Helen? Why the hell did you go inside the warehouse?"

"I was stupid. The man who took the money told me that my ex-husband was inside and wanted to straighten everything out in a friendly way. I was insane to believe that was even possible."

"No kidding."

"Don't you dare blame her," the senator growled.

Farber ignored him. "What happened once you got inside?"

"One of the men, the one who took the bag, was at least forty, and he had some sort of heavy accent, like Russian or Ukrainian. The other one looked like he was in his twenties and seemed afraid of the older man."

"What did they do to you?"

"As soon as we were inside, the one with the heavy accent grabbed me by the throat. He told me that I would have to make another payment to my ex-husband and that if I refused, it would be the last thing I ever did." She looked over at the senator and her eyes welled up with tears. "I'm so sorry, honey, so sorry."

The senator took her hand and shook his head. "Not important. You're alive. That's all that matters."

Farber was impatient. "And then?"

"Then we heard a shot from outside, and the older man with the accent dragged me away from the door and down an aisle between some wooden storage boxes. He told the younger one to get rid of me and then disappeared. I heard more gunfire, and the young guy looked like he was struggling to figure out what to do. Finally, he slugged me hard in the face, and I fell and almost passed out. One of the detectives, not Baker, came around the corner and saw us. He aimed a gun at the young guy and started to say something, but the man with the accent came up behind him and slammed something that looked like a small, black sock into the side of his head.

"A blackjack," Farber interjected. "Don't see those much anymore."

"Whatever it was, it must've been hard, because the detective fell to the ground and didn't move. They completely ignored me and started dragging the detective outside." She licked her lips. "Can I have some water please?"

Her husband quickly filled a glass and held it to her mouth. She managed one swallow and smiled at him. Helen's eyes were filled with pain. To Farber, she looked like a broken doll, grateful to not be abandoned.

"What about Sergeant Baker?" Lyle asked. "What happened to him?

"I don't know. I think they put both of them in the trunk of their car. I wanted to run, but I was too weak to move. I thought for sure they were going to kill me. But the young guy came back, picked me up, carried me out, and threw me in the back seat of the car. He leaned close and whispered to me that when he slowed down, I should throw myself out the door. He said if that I hesitated, I was dead. So, when it felt like we were heading up an onramp to the freeway, he did slow down, and I opened the door and jumped out. They couldn't stop because there were cars right behind them, thank God. In less than a minute, someone saw me waving and picked me up."

"You didn't hear them mention any names?" Farber had hoped for more. "Did they say anything about where they were going?"

"No, nothing that I could understand. The older man seemed to be in charge, and I could tell he was furious that everything had gone wrong."

Farber stood up, disappointed and angry. They had learned next to nothing.

Lyle leaned down and gave Helen a pat on her hand. "I'm happy you're alive and that you're going to be fine. Just rest, and if you think of anything, call us." He handed his card to the senator, who glared at him resentfully but took the card.

"She needs rest. She's told you all she can."

"Thank you." Helen whispered to Lyle. "This is my fault. I should have followed Sergeant Baker's instructions. If I had, none of this would have happened."

"Water under the bridge, Helen." Lyle assured her. "We'll find them."

Farber could barely contain his rage as headed out the door. "Water under the bridge, my ass," he said as they walked toward the elevators. "If my cops don't make it out of this alive, it's her damn fault." He punched the elevator button so hard Lyle was amazed it didn't break.

CHAPTER TEN

An hour out from Gilroy, Rosemaria's hands began to shake. She had to tighten her grip on the steering wheel to maintain control. Perspiration broke out on her forehead as doubts and questions began to assail her brain. What if Sidney Robbins wasn't at the family trailer? If she did catch him there, what if he wouldn't talk no matter how aggressively she threatened him? Should she just have let the cops handle him? And even if he did tell her where her father was, maybe it would be too late. She felt her usual self-confidence begin to dissipate.

She knew that there was little chance of street cameras being used to track her down. Once they had Sidney, they wouldn't waste hours of time trying to trace the movements of an unknown car and person, not even knowing where to start. But if her father were to be found alive, would the cops somehow figure out she'd been the person who coerced the information out of Sidney and then arrest her? Would her father forgive her if she caused him to lose the job that he loved? She took one hand off the steering wheel and wiped the perspiration out of her eyes. This kind of second-guessing was unacceptable. She had to pull herself together and keep her mind on the job she had set out to do. Concentrate. Focus. She had always been good at that.

Rosemaria hadn't wanted to push her luck by asking to talk to Mrs. Morgenstern's nephew to find out exactly where the Robbins's trailer was. She wouldn't want her having second thoughts and decide she'd better tell the police about the trailer after all. Not knowing where it was located meant Rosemaria would have to ask around for directions. She hated doing that, because the more people she talked to, the more chance there was that the police could track her down afterward. She wanted to avoid that at all costs.

She pulled off the freeway and headed toward downtown Gilroy, her heart pounding. If Sidney wasn't here, she would be devastated. Still wearing her now very wrinkled black suit, her black wig, and her sunglasses, she parked her car up the street from a 7-Eleven and its cameras, where she figured there would be some foot traffic. She stood by the side of her car, pretending to look at her phone, and waited for people to walk by on their way to the 7-Eleven. She questioned three passersby about where the Fillmore garlic-picker trailer park was before a nice, elderly Asian couple gave her directions.

She drove past the empty fields and easily found the trailer park. She parked on the side of a gravel road and changed into her baggy skirt and sweater. She added more dark makeup to her face and hands and put on her big straw hat and sunglasses. She wandered through the trailer park, trying to figure out exactly how she would find the right trailer. There weren't a lot of people living here in the off-season. Nevertheless, a Latino man whose face was weathered by sixty summers of hot sun knew the Robbins and where they lived. He told her there was no one in the trailer now, and she acted disappointed. She thanked the man and headed off in the direction of her car then doubled back and made her way to the Robbins's trailer.

As the Latino man had told her, it was the most run-down trailer in its row. She gasped as the trailer door opened and she found herself staring at a man who matched the photo of Sidney Robbins on his driver's license. He stepped down and turned to lock the trailer door. She made a quick about-face and walked between some trailers to another row, hoping he hadn't noticed her startled expression. He must be heading out to get something to eat close by. He couldn't risk driving his car on the freeway. She almost ran to her car. She needed to prepare.

* * * *

An hour later, Sidney came back to his trailer with a bagful of fruits and vegetables from a roadside stand. He didn't dare go to a store or park his car where there might be cameras. Every cop and sheriff in Southern California must be after him.

They'd told him that no one was supposed to get hurt. For sure no one was going to get shot. And now, here he was, hunted for being involved in the disappearance of two cops. Cops! They hadn't figured on cops showing up. What a total screwup. If they found the bodies his life was over.

He should have known better than do a job with Orlyk. He made the guy for a psycho the first time he'd laid eyes on him at a construction site where they'd both been working. He was a Ukrainian with a heavy accent and looked like he could shoot you as soon as look at you. But this job had seemed so simple—just take the money, hand it to some guy at a motel in Vernon and get paid two g's. Instead, Orlyk had gotten a weird look in his eyes when he'd seen the woman and talked her into coming into the warehouse. Sidney didn't know if Orlyk planned on threatening her, hurting her, or killing her. Then all hell broke loose. Maybe whoever hired them wanted the woman dead in the first place. Maybe Orlyk was just out of control and enjoyed killing for the hell of it. But Sidney couldn't shoot anybody and he sure as hell couldn't kill a woman. Orlyk said hiding the bodies meant they were free and clear. Obviously, he was a moron as well as a psycho. When the woman jumped out of the car, he thought Orlyk would have a fit. But Sidney was already in freeway traffic and there was nothing Orlyk could do about it.

He'd dumped a ranting, raving Orlyk off at his apartment in a sleazy neighborhood downtown, told him to keep the bag of money, and headed for Gilroy. He didn't want to be accused of stealing by the people who hired him. He was in enough trouble with them as it was. After everything that had happened, it had been way too dangerous to meet the guy in the motel and get paid. Now Sidney had hardly any money and would have to stay in the trailer for at least a month until things cooled down. Then he would drive to Mexico and never come back. The people who'd hired him would probably be after him as much as the police for botching a simple job. He unlocked the trailer door, not noticing the tiny scratch marks beside the lock. He stepped inside, shut the door, and felt a bottle break over his head. He stumbled, hit his head on the wall, and fell to the floor.

When Sidney came to, his head was throbbing. He was lying on his side, his hands and feet were hog-tied in front of him, and he was tied to the toilet. He couldn't move. He could barely breathe because his mouth was taped shut. He was in a nightmare, but he had no idea who had put him here. Had the people who hired him found him somehow? If it was them, he was dead for sure. He heard footsteps coming close and looked up to see an apparition standing before him, holding a gun that was aimed down at the floor. The person was covered in black from head to toe. The eyes were covered by sunglasses. When the apparition spoke, Sidney's blood ran cold. The voice was garbled and low.

Rosemaria looked down at the frightened man on the floor and felt nothing but absolute calm. "You are going to tell me where you took the police officers, who you are working for, and who your partner is, or I will kill you. Do you understand?"

She ripped the tape off his mouth. "If you scream, I will shoot." She took the silencer out of her pocket and screwed it onto the Beretta.

Sidney shook until he thought his teeth would rattle. Tell the apparition what he knew? Give up Orlyk and tell her who hired them? That would be a death sentence for him. Maybe the apparition would only hurt him.

"I don't know who hired us. It was over the phone. We weren't supposed to kill anybody, I swear."

The black figure fired the gun, and the bullet missed his foot by an inch. Wood and tile exploded and splintered into his leg. He began to babble.

"I went to the warehouse with a foreign guy, Orlyk—Ukrainian, I think. I met him at a construction site, and he told me we could make some easy money. We met a guy at an abandoned dock in San Pedro who told us what we had to do. He had an accent too; I think it was Ukrainian like Orlyk's. We were supposed to deliver the money to him at a motel in Vernon, and he was going to pay us there. But then everything went south, and I ran."

"What I would like to know—and I will not repeat my question again—is where did you take the police officers? I will make a call and wait to find out if you're telling the truth, and if you're lying to me, the next bullet will find your heart."

Sidney could feel the sweat pouring off his forehead and into his eyes. "We took them to the old subway construction site, two exits south of Vernon, that was abandoned ten years ago. There's a deep pit there that goes down to where they started putting in the rails. We threw them in there." Desperate to earn some good will, Sydney added, "We let the woman go right away!"

"Good for you, Sydney. Are the police officers alive?"

Sidney hesitated, afraid to tell the truth. "I...don't know. Orlyk shot them both before throwing them in the pit."

Rosemaria slapped the tape back on his mouth. Hearing her father had been shot almost took her breath away. She walked into the living area of the trailer and grabbed Sidney's cell phone from where he had it plugged in to charge the battery. She had realized just in time that she couldn't use her burner to call both 911 and Farber. They could find out later that the same phone had made both calls. Thank God Sidney still had his cell and the trailer had electricity.

She walked back to where Sydney was tied up, ripped off the tape and gave him precise instructions on what to say to the 911 operator. She dialed and held the phone to his mouth. Sweating profusely, Sydney gave the operator the information regarding where the pit was located and told her that two cops may be lying at the bottom of the pit, dying, and needed immediate help. Rosemaria yanked the phone away, clicked it off and refastened the tape on Sydney's mouth. She would wait half an hour and call Farber. She'd be in trouble later if they bothered to track the location of the burner call. She didn't know if they could even do that, but she'd be shocked if they went to the trouble. No reason at all to do it. She was the daughter of the victim. Meanwhile, her heart was beating so hard it felt like it would explode out of her chest.

* * * *

Two times Steven thought he heard noises up above. He called out and waved his flashlight, but no one came. He tried to relax and conserve his energy. He had one bite left of his Snickers bar and decided to save it for later. His eyelids felt heavy, and it took tremendous will to keep his eyes open and stay alert. He felt himself sinking into unconsciousness, then, in a split second, he was wide awake. He thought he heard something—voices, footsteps. He was sure of it. He turned on his flashlight and waved it back and forth. He saw the face of a uniformed officer in the bright space far above. "I'm here!" he yelled with a voice that was really only a whisper. "I'm here!"

* * * *

Rosemaria, took a deep breath and said a quick prayer. She opened the door slightly, looked around to make sure no one was around, then stepped outside and called Farber on her burner. "Has my dad been found yet?"

"Yes, he's on his way to the hospital. He's in bad shape but nothing life threatening. Messina, sad to say, is dead. How did you—"

Rosemaria clicked off, went back inside, filled her mouth with tissue and pebbles again, cut off a new bit of masking tape and grabbed Sydney's cell phone off the counter. When she knelt and reached for the tape covering his mouth he cringed. It hurt like hell every time she tore it off, which, unfortunately, she did again. "Tell the operator who and where you are, that you are tied up and will surrender peacefully." She dialed 911 and held the phone to his mouth. Sydney did as he was told.

Rosemaria pressed the fresh masking tape on his mouth. "Don't try to loosen the rope or tape. They're on tight. When the police come, you will tell them everything you know about the crime you committed."

She used her small knife to dig the bullet she had fired next to his foot out of the floor. She didn't waste another look at Sidney.

Sidney was so relieved, he wanted to cry. But he knew he better not, because then his nose would plug up and he wouldn't be able to breathe. He would tell the police every last detail of what he knew. Anything was better than dealing with the black apparition.

Rosemaria went back to the living area, spit the tissue and pebbles out of her mouth, ripped off her ski cap, unzipped her ski cover-up, and tore it off. She changed into her jeans and T-shirt and stuffed the other clothes and supplies into her backpack. She decided to take Sidney's phone for good measure. Then she peeked out the door. The row of trailers was still deserted. She walked quickly to her car and put everything in her trunk. She pulled apart her burner phone and Sydney's phone, crushed them to pieces in the dirt, and picked them up. She drove through town until she reached a deserted homeless encampment where she had previously spied an oil drum used to make fires in at night to keep the homeless warm. She threw her skirt, sweater, hat, wig, and all the supplies she had brought into the drum and, lastly, tore off her gloves before pouring lighter fluid over everything and dropping in a lit match. She waited a few nervous minutes, constantly making sure no one was nearby, while the contents burned, then, after she was certain the fire had consumed it all, she headed back to Simi.

At home, after emptying the Beretta of bullets, she placed the gun back in the safe, along with the suppressor, not wanting to take the time to clean it, knowing her father probably wouldn't check the Beretta until months from now. By then, he wouldn't be able to tell it had been fired. She took her own cell phone from where she had left it in her desk and saw that Farber had left her several messages. She needed to have a good reason why it took her over four hours to get to her father's side at the hospital. She'd think of something on the way.

* * * *

When Steven opened his eyes, it felt like déjà vu. His daughter's face was looking down on him, just a foot away. She smiled just as she had smiled down at him at his bedside almost nine years ago. Her green eyes glowed with happiness, just as they had glowed then. He struggled to speak. She had to lean down close to hear him.

"I'm sorry, daughter. I caused you so much trouble."

She sat back up and patted his hand. "I'm just glad you're safe, Dad. I had all the faith in the world that Farber, Lyle, and the others would find you."

He closed his eyes again and slept, knowing all was well with the world.

* * * *

They were in the backyard at the picnic table, sharing a pizza and coke. Rosemaria had just aced another exam and it had made her ravenous.

Her father chewed his slice thoughtfully. "Losing Messina was hard. He was a good cop."

"I really liked him. He was always nice to me. What you said at his funeral was beautiful."

"Slim comfort to his wife and two kids."

"What happened wasn't your fault, Dad."

"I was an idiot. I should have been prepared for things to go sideways. I was too complacent."

"Dad, you're just going to have to admit you're not perfect."

"You're perfect."

"I tend to be obsessive-compulsive like you, but not quite perfect."

"It's good to be that way. Tying up loose ends when you're a cop preparing a case for the prosecution you can't leave any stone unturned."

Rosemaria was startled. *What the heck did he know? What had he and Farber been discussing?* "I hear Sidney gave up Orlyk, and Orlyk copped a plea and gave up Sandusky and his Ukrainian connections."

"The Ukrainians wanted Orlyk to scare Helen out of her wits to convince her to stay away from the cops and not expose Sandusky's criminal connections with them. They needed Sandusky to stay in business to keep bleeding him dry. Sandusky just thought he could neutralize Helen and blackmail her into giving him the money to keep his construction projects going."

"I almost feel sorry for him. He was getting hit from all sides."

"Not too sorry. He did have Clemente murdered, and Messina is dead because of him. With Helen's testimony, it looks like Sandusky will finally get what's coming to him."

"Not to mention you handing the Ukrainians over to the feds so they can unravel that whole mess."

"Farber told me you had been following your own clues to try and find me and ended up in San Pedro."

Rosemaria's heart stopped. She didn't like lying to her father, but she couldn't tell him the truth and make him part of her criminal behavior. It could ruin his career. "Ah, yeah. Obviously, I should have left it to the professionals."

"Turned out it was a tip called in by somebody up in Gilroy who knew where Sidney was hiding and got him to talk."

"Most cases are solved by tips."

"Somebody had tied him up pretty good."

"Do they know the identity of that person?"

"Nope. Could have been somebody with a grudge against him. We'll probably never know. Sidney had an interesting story to tell but it's probably a bunch of BS. At any rate, nobody's looking, and the department's moved on. The prosecutor is dealing with Sandusky. Our job is done."

Rosemaria almost breathed a sigh of relief but stopped herself.

"Not all investigations are by the book, you know," her father added.

"No?"

"Sometimes you have to fly off the reservation and do what's necessary. I've done it a couple of times myself."

"Well, if I ever decide to become a cop, I'll remember that."

"Just protect the people you work with. That's important."

She struggled to keep a smile off her face. *He knew everything!* "I can do that."

"I'm sure you can, daughter. I'd stake my life on it."

Oh yeah, he knew. She grabbed another piece of pizza, thinking of the choices she had to make soon. She was pretty certain of the path she would take. She patted her father's arm and took a big bite of her slice.

THE END

Britt Lind is an actress, singer, and writer who has performed in television shows, movies, and on stage in Los Angeles, New York, and Vancouver, BC. She has written several screenplays and came in as runner-up in the Washington State Screenwriting Competition for her screenplay *A Light in the Forest*. Britt lives in Thousand Oaks, California with her husband, Nick Alexander, a screenwriter, and their three feral cats, Teeny, Toughie, and Baby Hughie who used to live a hardscrabble life in the cold and rain in the frozen north of Washington State and now enjoy a life of luxury in the sun, as is their due. Britt is also president of a nonprofit, People for Reason in Science and Medicine, a pro-health, pro-environment, anti-vivisection organization. Her inspirational memoir *Learning How to Fly*, which was a winner in the 2019 Beverly Hills Book Awards in the performing arts category, is available on Amazon. Her website is www.brittlind.com.

To find out more about PRISM, please go to
www.peopleforreason.org and www.facebook.com/gotoprism
Follow PRISM on Twitter @gotoprism

CPSIA information can be obtained
at www.ICGtesting.com
Printed in the USA
LVHW030020010322
712228LV00004B/270